Persi and the Lost Soul

Nancy Harman

Copyright © 2012 Nancy Harman

All rights reserved.

ISBN:10 1542814359
ISBN-13: 978-1542814355

DEDICATION

I would like to dedicate this book to my mum,

Margaret Marshall

ACKNOWLEDGEMENTS

Thanks go once again to John for originally encouraging me to write, Jo for proof reading and Sarah for posting me the proof when it came as I was out cruising around the canals. I am blessed with my family and friends.

Chapter 1

Persi still visited the museum whenever she could to see 'her' necklace and its two sister pendants. The thrill never went away and her senses were always heightened after seeing them. She always went on her own, she knew that Danny would have gone with her but she somehow preferred to be on her own. She could tell that sometimes other people gave her funny looks when she spent the best part of an hour in front of their case, not really looking at anything else, but each time she was remembering her dreams and how they each gave her a bit more knowledge until finally the mystery was solved.

Occasionally she wished she could have just kept the two that she had found and not given them up to be reunited with the final pendant but deep down she knew that that hadn't been an option. They had to be together and she was the one they chose to get the job done. She still wondered why it was her, but once she was in front of them and felt their power filling her up again, she knew that for some reason they had chosen correctly, she had been the right choice, and she would leave with an enigmatic smile on her face, knowing that she truly was 'special' in some way.

She had gone back to school that September and discovered a new friend. Neda and her twin brother Moj had moved into one of the new houses on Gunners Field and they were in the same year as her. Neda was quiet and shy but since Persi had been pretty much abandoned by Abby, she made a special effort to be friendly and it had worked. They were in most classes together and on the nights that Persi went to stay with her Grandma, Neda often went around and learnt to love the garden. To say nothing of discovering the delights of Grandmas cooking!

Persi would go to Neda's home sometimes and enjoyed the smells and flavours that their mum would combine to produce meals unlike anything that Persi had tried before. Neda's mum was even quieter than she was but her dad was quite friendly and liked having others come around. There were three younger siblings, two boys who were just typical annoying little brothers and a toddler who won Persi's heart with her huge brown eyes and big smile.

She and Danny spent a fair bit of their time together, not just because of their parents now seeing each other more and more often, but because they shared a love of the canal, boats and Grandma. When she was with Danny she felt that she could be completely honest, since he knew all about her necklaces and had been a great help in putting all the pieces of the jigsaw together. He also couldn't forget how Persi had 'healed' his aches and pains when he'd tripped over a toy his dog Daisy had left on the stairs. That had really been the beginning of their friendship.

Persi hadn't told Neda about the whole necklace adventure as it seemed all a bit distant now and she didn't want to run the risk of losing another friend thinking she was weird just because she had 'real' dreams. In any case nothing had happened since she had donated the pendants to the museum so she thought that all of that was behind her. She had to admit to herself though that she felt different after visiting the necklaces and believed that she still had the capacity to heal or at least help relieve pain. She'd accepted she was a bit different but wasn't going to let it rule her life. She was quite happy the way she was, although she was beginning to think that a new adventure would be nice, life seemed very quiet now that she'd left the Vikings behind!

One Saturday just before half term Neda and Moj had gone to visit some family so she and Danny went off to the market to see what was around and to just enjoy some of Danny's time off. He was now helping out quite regularly at the boatyard and his dad was even paying him for some of the jobs. They were wandering around the stalls when she felt a sensation similar to the one that she had when her swan had been trying to tell her something. A heaviness and tingling started in her fingers and spread throughout her body.

"What's up?" Danny had noticed her stopping and seeming to be lost in thought.

"I don't know." She looked at him nervously, "I just had the most peculiar sensation. As if something was trying to find me."

"What sort of something?" Danny looked bemused.

"No idea." She looked around her and realised that they were stopped beside a stall selling bric-a-brac. "Maybe there's something here."

Danny looked worried. "Perce, not again, please. You don't know what you might be getting into." He grabbed her hand and tried to pull her away.

She wrenched her hand away. "No, I can't leave, you go if you like but there's something here that needs me."

Danny reluctantly came back and together they looked around at the items that were spread out across an old shawl, disguising the trestle table underneath. Cautiously Persi ran her hand across the smaller items, until an undeniable connection was made. A ring, silver, small, quite undistinguished looking, with a single brownish blue stone in it was calling unmistakably to her.

The man behind the counter spotted her and immediately looked at her hand, as if she was trying to steal something.

"Anything special you want love?"

"No, not really. This ring, do you know anything about it?"

"Nah, just came in a box of jewellery, £5 to you darling."

"Oh no thank you, I don't have that much, no I was only just looking."

As she turned away, she felt a sharp stabbing pain in her head. She KNEW it was the ring calling her.

"How about £4, if you like it, hey?" The stallholder called after her.

Danny turned back to him. "I've got £3.50, take it or leave it, I think my friend likes it but it's not really that special is it?"
Persi couldn't bear to turn around to see what was happening. The physical sensations were so strong, she knew she really had to have the ring, even if she had to borrow some money from her mum or grandma.

"OK then, I suppose I can let it go, it's been quiet today and I don't want to take it all back with me." He picked up the ring and gave it to Danny who handed over the money in change.

They walked away and Danny put the ring in Persi's hand.

Immediately the pain in her head eased, to be replaced by a warm, tingling glow that she couldn't believe others weren't able to see.

Persi smiled up at Danny. "Thank you so much, I'll pay you back, but I had to have it, really."

"Don't be soft, you don't have to pay it back. Dad paid me today, so it's not a problem. Just be careful won't you Perce, let me help if you need me?"

"Thanks, and of course I'll ask you to help if I need it. I haven't got a clue what's going to happen with this but I know the ring wanted me to have it." She smiled up at him and started to wonder if this was the beginning of another adventure. The swan necklace had a definite connection with her and was able to show her through dreams what it wanted her to do. She presumed that the ring was going to be much the same.

She was still holding it in her hand, so without thinking she moved it onto her finger. Everything went black.

Chapter 2

Persi found herself in a dark and frankly unpleasant forest. She could sense shapes around her and nothing felt friendly. She became aware of animal noises, snuffing and snorting around and hoped that they would avoid her. The dogs in the Viking settlement had raised their hackles and run at the sight of her, she fervently hoped that these would react in the same way.

An unpleasant smell wafted towards her and she felt more scared than she'd ever been before. What on earth was out there?

"Ha, another lost soul for her to catch." A small, aged voice appeared to come from a tree in front of her.

"I've no idea what you mean, I don't know where I am or what I'm doing here." She tried to sound confident and assertive, but was afraid that she'd sounded terrified, which she was.

"No-one chooses to come here. You are lost, believe me." A small, wizened old lady appeared from behind the tree and stared at Persi. "What's your name child?"

"Persephone." She managed to say. It didn't seem the sort of place to be called Persi. Her full name added more gravitas she felt.

"Persephone you say? How appropriate, goddess of the underworld, and a reluctant one at that. You are well named."

"What is this place?" Persi was seriously worried by now and felt that what she'd just heard didn't make her feel any less anxious.

"Doesn't matter much, does it! You're here and unlikely to leave, so you'll have plenty of time to discover it for yourself." With that she laughed and seemed to disappear amongst the trees.

Now much as Persi hadn't liked having the old lady there, somehow being on her own was much worse. The sounds of the forest became more pronounced and she took a few deep breaths before considering her next move.

It was obvious that wherever she was, it wasn't the here and now that she was used to. Neither did it feel like her previous dreams had done. Then she was aware of everything around her but somehow not a part of it. This felt much more solid, and the fact that the old lady had spoken to her as if she was real, made it all the more frightening. It felt like a long way away both in time and place. It was dark, but she didn't know if that meant it was night-time or whether it was just that the forest was so overgrown above her that no light was coming through. Slowly she realised that there WAS light, just not the sort of daylight that she'd have expected. It was almost as if some of the plants had a sort of phosphorescence because as her eyes grew used to it, she realised that she could see quite a bit, in an eerie sort of way.

She noticed that just a couple of feet away was a sort of track, just an animal run, barely noticeable unless you were scared, alone, lost and desperate. Persi ticked all of these boxes and was delighted to spot it. She figured that if animals used it, it was unlikely to take her over a cliff or into a gully, and might lead to water. That said, she also wondered what sort of animals used it. Hopefully as it was a small track, it would be small animals. Rabbits were what she was hoping for. She could cope with rabbits!

Tentatively she climbed over the brambles between her and the path and decided that she'd turn to the right. It took her a moment to realise that she was able to touch and feel things in this place. That was something else that was different. She briefly remembered trying to pick up the necklace when it was dropped and not being able to. That feeling of helplessness was now replaced by one of pain. She was definitely able to feel these brambles and nettles. The left path didn't look as easy to follow, so that decided her to go right. Cautiously, testing the ground before putting her weight down, she went a few feet. Nothing terrible had happened so she became a bit bolder. She walked, slowly but steadily along the path and realised that she was going downhill, very gradually. After a while, time seemed difficult to measure in the semi-darkness and the oppressive air, not moving amongst the trees, made it rather unreal, she came to a clearing. The sound of water suddenly reached her senses and she held back a sob. At least if she had water she wouldn't die here, at least not for a while.

"Stop, who dares to enter my home?" The deep, gravelly voice came from nowhere and Persi jumped, suddenly realising how stupid she'd been, wandering around an obviously hostile forest, without thinking about the consequences.

"I'm sorry, I didn't realise it was anyone's home, I'm just trying to find my way out of here."

The laughter cut her short, it was mean and nasty, the sort that wasn't funny at all, just threatening. "No-one gets out of here. This is now where you live, but NOT here, this is mine."

Persi allowed herself to get cross now. "How dare you, I WILL get out, and I've no intention of living here, it's foul, it stinks and I don't belong here." With that she did what turned out to be another stupid thing, she turned and ran back in the general direction that she'd come from. The laughter followed her.

In no time at all she found herself imprisoned in brambles, stung by the most malevolent stinging nettles she'd ever encountered, and no-where near the path that she'd come along before. Determined not to cry she started getting herself disentangled from the thorns and once free she looked around for some dock leaves. Luckily even in such an overwhelmingly unpleasant place as the forest she found herself in, there were still docks growing nearby. Methodically she pulped the large leaves up and applied them to the stings on her ankles and all up her arms. As the stinging sensation gradually went away, she gave in and started to weep. Gently at first and then, not caring who or what heard her, she gave way to huge, gulping sobs, that wracked her whole body.

Once she'd got that out of her system she finally remembered the ring she was wearing. It hadn't affected her at all since she'd put it on and presumably landed herself in this place. There was no tingling or temperature change or anything that gave her any clues as to what she ought to do. She tried to take it off, but as she did so, it seemed to tighten its grip on her finger and she realised that for some reason it wanted her to stay where she was. But where was she, what was she meant to do and how could she get away?

Chapter 3

Slowly and carefully Persi moved away from the brambles towards an area that looked less dense than the rest and once again heard the welcome sound of water. Another couple of steps and she almost fell into the stream that was running past. Tentatively she put her hand in and scooped up a mouthful of water. It was icy cold and tasted remarkably pleasant, considering everything else she'd come across in this strange place. She'd half expected to be spitting out the mouthful she'd taken, but no it was rather nice and so she gratefully drank her fill and sat down on a nearby rock to consider what she should do next.

A soft voice, surprisingly pleasant, came to her. "Thank you, I think you've come for me." She looked around and saw a young boy, about 9 years old, gazing at her from the other side of the stream.

"I'm sorry, what did you say?" Persi wasn't sure she'd heard and it was so nice to hear someone talk gently to her that she had taken more notice of the tone than the words.

"I said thank you. I've been here for ages waiting for someone to come and find me. I want to get home to my mother, and I think she sent you."

"What makes you say that?" Persi was mystified, knowing that no-one had sent her and also wondering how he could have been here for ages, surely someone would have come to find him?

"You're wearing my mother's ring, the one my father gave her."

Persi looked down and saw the ring positively glowing and now she thought about it, she could feel it loosening the hold on her finger and feeling warmer.

"Your mothers ring? Oh, I see. Well she didn't exactly give it to me, I bought it and now I'm here. I'm not sure what's happening but I don't know how to save myself let alone you. But at least we can be together now to work it all out." She smiled at the boy, hoping that he would understand, even though she didn't have a clue herself.

She was surprised at his reaction. He went red in the face and started screaming at her. "You stole it, my mother would never sell her ring, it's too special to her. You're a thief, I hope you die in the forest. Now I shall never get home." With that he ran off, obviously knowing the path he was taking as he didn't stumble or falter on his way.

"No wait, wait, I didn't steal it, honestly." Persi ran after him, trying to follow his tracks but he quickly outran her and she was left alone. The only good thing was that the ring seemed to have stayed loose on her finger and quickly she pulled it off.

She came to on a bench near the market, surrounded by the sort of crowd that always appear when someone falls over or has some sort of minor accident. Not there to help, just to see what all the bother is about. She looked into Danny's face and saw the worry there.

"Hello you." He said with a distinct note of fear. She smiled at him.

He looked around at the people and said, none too nicely. "It's OK, she's fine now, you can all go away, we're good." Slowly the crowd dispersed and in the meantime, Danny looked back at Persi.

"OK, give me back that ring."

"No, no I can't. It's telling me something." Persi was scared at the expression on Danny's face.

"Look it's all very well you saying that. I was bloody terrified. You put the ring on and just passed out, your pulse went to practically zero, you started to go cold, I thought you were going to die. You just can't play around with this sort of stuff."

Persi could see he was really upset, but she knew she couldn't just abandon the child she'd met in the forest. If he'd been stuck there it was somehow down to her to help him. She had no idea how she'd do it and the idea of returning to the forest scared her witless, but she knew she couldn't abandon him.

"We'll talk about this later. I really need a drink and a bun or something now, please Danny?" She looked up at him, trying to make him understand that she needed some time.

"OK but don't you DARE put that ring on again, certainly not on your own. Honest Perce, you terrified me."

They walked off a little way and found a stall selling drinks and doughnuts so they returned to the bench and ate and drank in silence, both lost in their own thoughts.

After a while, Danny stood up. "OK, we're going to see your grandma, she'll know what to do. You're not going to meddle in something that is going to hurt you. She'll agree, I know she will."

Persi had a horrible feeling that he was right but since he sounded much calmer now, she thought it was probably easiest to go along with his suggestion. In any case she was more scared that she wanted Danny to know and thought that the comfort of grandma's house would be welcome.

Chapter 4

They caught the bus and got off at Henbury, the small village where grandma lived, and made their way to her house. Persi suddenly wondered if she'd be at home or whether she'd be off at one of her fundraising 'do's'. Maybe they should have rung first.

As it turned out, grandma was just arriving home as they turned the corner.

"How lovely to see you both, to what do I owe this pleasure?" Grandma spoke as she opened the door and let them all in.

Before Persi could get a word in Danny breathlessly answered. "She's up to it again, Perse got a ring in the market and when she put it on she went out cold. I thought she was going to die. You've got to stop her using it again, it's going to hurt her. I know it is."

Grandma stopped in her tracks and looked back at the two of them. Seeing Persi's expression and the fear in Danny's face worried her but first things first she thought.

"Right come on through to the kitchen, I'll put a kettle on and you can both tell me what's happened,"

Ten minutes later they were sat around the table with a cup of something warm. Grandma and Persi had camomile tea and Danny had elected for coffee, not yet quite used to grandma's passion for making her own herbal teas. They had both declined cake since the doughnuts in the market were pretty big.

Both of them told their versions of what had happened and grandma looked seriously worried by the end of it.

"I think that Danny's right for now, would you let me keep the ring for the time being until we work out what to do about it." She noticed Persi's expression. "Don't worry, we're not going to abandon it, but I feel that I need to do some thinking about this and maybe discuss it with someone who may know more about it than I do. Don't ask!" She saw the questions in both of their faces. "You'll have to trust me in this. Will you let me have it Persephone, just for the time being?"

Persi knew when she was beaten, and reluctantly got it out of her pocket and handed it over. She noticed the relief in Danny's face, but also caught a strange expression in her grandma's face as she took the ring in her hand.

"What is it? You felt something didn't you?"

Grandma nodded. "There is definitely something strange about the ring, but leave it with me and I'll let you know how I'm getting on. In the meantime, what else has been going on?"

They had a difficult, halting conversation about school and what their parents were up to. Over the summer Danny's dad Robbie and Persi's mum Donna, had got together and it was becoming obvious that they were serious about each other. Everyone was delighted with the situation and once the awkwardness of it all had disappeared, life had much improved for all of them. So they spoke about this and that and then Danny realised that the light was beginning to go so they said their goodbyes and walked off along the tow path towards their homes.

Chapter 5

That night on the narrow boat where they lived, Persi had a chat with her mum about what had happened, because she thought it would be better coming from her than from either of the others. Mum was concerned naturally, but pleased that Danny had been sensible enough to take Persi to her grandma's and she knew that between them they wouldn't let Persi do anything stupid.

That night Persi checked online what the story of Persephone was, as she wanted to know what the old woman had meant by being goddess of the underworld. She found that Persephone had been kidnapped while picking flowers and was taken to be the bride of Orpheus god of the underworld. All a bit scary but only a legend when all was said and done. She didn't feel as if it was connected to her at all and dismissed it.

She tried to look up information about silver rings but there was so much and she had so little information that it was hopeless. She then remembered the strange brownish blue stone and looked that up. She thought that it was most likely to be Blue John, a fairly rare stone that had been mined in the past about 20 miles away from them. It was definitely found in the Midlands so she realised that there could be a local connection. That was lucky she thought, like finding that the Vikings had settled in the area made finding the necklaces easier she hoped this would be similar. She couldn't forget though how different this experience had been. She could feel and smell and others could see her and they were able to speak to each other. Those facts made this seem very different and although Persi had wished that those people in her previous dreams could have heard her and that she could have touched things, now that it was happening she wasn't so sure it was a good thing.

She spent a long time thinking about everything that she'd seen or heard. Nothing made sense. Picturing the boy again she realised that he was wearing clothes that had probably been around for hundreds of years amongst the poorer classes many years ago. A sort of brown linen tunic with leather sandals. She hadn't thought it strange at the time but now she realised that he might have been there, in that awful place for years. And yet he was still young. Where WAS the place? Did it exist alongside now, like a sort of parallel universe? Had she gone back to a snapshot in time like she had before in her dreams? That whole episode seemed so simple now. She got given a necklace, it took her through a range of dreams until she found its sister necklaces. Job done. What on earth was this ring all about?

She wished that she still had it but knew that if she did, she wouldn't be able to stop herself putting it on again, and could she cope with whatever happened next?

Eventually she fell into a restless sleep and dreamt about being tied up in ropes that would never undo, and trees that kept laughing at her and trying to trip her up. It was a relief to wake up and she spent the day doing chores and homework in a tired daze. Neda rang late afternoon for a chat but Persi let her natter on, not contributing much to the conversation, eventually apologising and blaming a bad headache, promising to see her on the bus in the morning.

Within ten minutes of ending the call, and just as Persi decided to have a shower and go to bed early since Mum was out having a drink with Robbie, her phone went and she was surprised to see it was grandma.

"Hello darling, is this a good time to talk?"

"Perfect, a few minutes later and I wouldn't have heard the phone, but I'm all yours now."

"Right well I have a friend, her name is Rita, and she's very good at understanding…. well shall we say, unusual items. Our mothers knew each other and used to help each other out when necessary."

Persi read between the lines of this and realised that Rita was another 'wise woman' as her grandma would call her, or witch as some others might!

"OK, that's nice, so what's going to happen?"

"Well it so happens that Rita will be in the area next week, and specifically will be free on Wednesday afternoon. She's going to come for tea with me and I wondered if you'd like to come over and meet her. She thinks she might be able to help us with the ring."

"That's amazing, I haven't stopped thinking about it and I was half expecting you to refuse me to have anything to do with it. Thank you so much grandma, I do love you!"

"Now hold on, there might not be anything that can be done. If Rita says you're to have nothing to do with it then that has to be final Persephone. I know of no one who can help us more with this. You have to trust me on this."

Persi took a deep breath. This wasn't exactly what she wanted to hear. What if the boy was going to be imprisoned in that awful place for the rest of eternity? Could she live with that? What choice did she have though? Grandma, her mum, Danny and even Robbie would all be on the same side, they'd all want to protect her. There were times she HATED being 13. Reluctantly she answered her grandma in the only possible way.

"OK, I'll do as you and Rita say, I promise."

"Good girl, just come around after school as usual and you can stay if you like."

"Thanks, that would be lovely, see you then."

Once off the phone, Persi started wondering who this Rita was and what did her grandma mean by saying she was in the area next weekend? Grandma had always lived around here and she'd never mentioned a Rita before.

She had her shower and went to bed with a light, silly book and fell asleep just as her mum came home. Her dreams that night were a lot less dramatic and she awoke the next day ready to get to school and face the world.

Chapter 6

On the bus the next day she managed to tell Danny the basic conversation she'd had with Grandma before Neda and Moj got on. Neda sat in front of Persi and immediately turned to the two of them and said excitedly.

"Have you seen the posters? There's a fair coming to the field next to our estate and it's going to open on Thursday with cheap tickets. There's a poster by our bus-stop. Moj and I are going, do you two want to come with us?"

"Great idea!" Danny responded immediately. "That would be fun, wouldn't it Persi?"

"Yes as long as I don't have to go on too many rides! I'm up for as much candy-floss and toffee apples as you can force down me though!"

They spent the rest of the journey discussing the fair and Persi enjoyed just being a teenager, chatting away to her friends. Life was good and whatever Wednesday held in store, she'd deal with it.

The next few days went by with the usual round of lessons, homework and chores. The weather had started to turn a lot colder and they were all hoping that the rain that they had been getting overnight wouldn't make the fairground too muddy and also that it would stay dry for their outing. Persi was pleased that she was seeing grandma on Wednesday this week as she usually stayed there on Thursday nights and so it all worked out well for her.

Mum was happy that Persi had been sensible in promising grandma that she would abide by Rita's decision. She had told Persi that she vaguely remembered hearing the name Rita when she was a child, but she couldn't put a face to the name, so Persi was still wondering who this strange woman would turn out to be.

Wednesday finally arrived and Persi got off the bus with Neda and Moj, explaining to Neda that her grandma had a visitor so she couldn't invite her around that evening, then walked along the lane to her grandma's house.

She went in as usual, dropping her bag inside the door, hanging her coat up and calling out. "Hello, I'm here!"

She walked into the kitchen and there sat at the table was one of the plainest women Persi had ever seen. She wasn't ugly, just completely forgettable. The sort of person that if you had to describe you would just say 'average'. She would disappear into a crowd with no difficulty, somehow Persi had expected something a bit more dramatic.

"Persephone, there you are! Come in and meet my good friend Rita."

Rita got up and gave Persi a hug, then held her away at arm's length and said. "Mmmm. You are just as I expected. Welcome Persephone, I think we can work together over this."

Feelings of relief were uppermost in Persi's mind, but also wondering about what a strange greeting this had been. She smiled in reply and returned the hug.

"Cup of tea anyone?" Grandma broke the tension as usual with a spot of normality. The others laughed and both agreed that a cup of tea would be welcome.

They were soon sat around the table and Persi was painfully aware that there was a box in the centre of the table that she could tell held the ring. She could feel the waves reaching out from it to her, calling her. The urge to reach out and touch it was almost unbearable yet she knew that if she did it would be the wrong thing to do and might jeopardise the possible help she was going to get from these two lovely ladies.

She looked up eventually and saw them looking at each other with a glance that told her she'd passed the first test.

Rita broke the silence.

"This ring, can you tell me exactly how you found it?"

Thinking carefully, Persi explained how she had felt it calling out to her from the market stall and how she had become its owner, or rather how it had become her owner.

"Good, so there is no doubt that it wanted you. Your grandma has explained how you managed to locate the necklaces, and this tells me that you have extremely rare talents. For your age, you are truly remarkable. Indeed for our age you would certainly stand out as exceptional." She smiled at grandma who nodded back to her.

Persi had heard similar from her great-grandmother in her first 'real' dream, yet she was still embarrassed by hearing it said and unsure as to how she should respond. She settled for looking down at her hands, which were clenched tightly together to avoid her reaching out towards the ring.

She looked up. "So where do we go from here? I feel really strongly that I ought to go back and find the boy I saw. I just feel that it's my job somehow. I know I promised to do whatever you said Rita but I just feel this need."

Grandma started to say something but Rita interrupted her. "Of course you must…" Before she could say anything else Persi burst into tears and said, "Thank you, thank you SO much."

"Wait, not so fast. This is very dangerous territory you want to go to. You cannot do it alone. I can offer you some advice as to how to make it safer……. but listen, and listen very carefully. You must never, on ANY account try to do it yourself again. It could be fatal."

Persi went pale. Up to now it had just seemed something rather nasty that she had to do, but she'd never really considered it to be THAT dangerous. Looking at Rita, such an ordinary, nondescript person, she suddenly saw the depth and importance behind her words. Fatal. Nothing had prepared her for that. She still wanted to do it, she thought she did anyway, but should she? She knew what Danny and her mum would say. Could she do it? Deep down she knew she could and indeed that she would, but there were so many problems in her way.

Looking up at both her grandma and Rita she made her decision.

"OK, what do I have to do then?"

Grandma laughed, "I knew that would be your response, oh Persephone, what an amazing girl you are. Mother was so right about you."

Rita looked serious. "I shall think this through carefully and I need to prepare some items. I will let your grandma know what needs to be done by the beginning of next week. Whatever she tells you, you MUST do. You have many people caring for you and you need to remember how precious you are. Persephone, this will not be easy but I believe that you will succeed. If I had doubts I wouldn't let you do this, believe me."

Persi felt a thrill go down her spine. Whatever happened from now on, she knew that she'd be safe. She didn't know how or why she could put her trust in this stranger, but she did, and somehow it felt comforting.

"I shall have to take the ring with me to ensure that what I prepare is correct." she looked at Persi. "You can trust me."

"I know, thank you so much, I'm so grateful for your help. I know that this is the right thing to do." She got up and gave Rita a hug that crushed the air out of her.

Rita looked across at grandma, "Right I must be off now. I shall be in touch. Thank you for your lovely tea, I always look forward to it. Persephone, put all thoughts of the ring out of your mind as much as you can. It won't help to dwell on it and you need to be as relaxed and happy as you can. It's very strong you know, the gift of happiness and love, and I can see you are surrounded by it."

Persi felt unaccountably emotional and hugged Rita again, kissing her on the cheek this time.

"Goodbye and thank you so much, I'm truly grateful to you."

At that Rita collected her coat and carefully put the ring, inside its box, into her bag and said her goodbyes to grandma and went off down the lane.

"Is she staying locally then?" Persi asked.

"Oh yes, not far at all. Right then, after all of that I thought a nice casserole would do us good."

Persi became aware of the wonderful smells that were coming from the oven and wondered how she hadn't noticed them before. They sat down and were soon tucking into large plates of beef and dumplings in a rich and tasty gravy. They cleared up afterwards and had a lovely evening not talking about the ring but going through photo albums and remembering places and people from their past, and discussing what plants Grandma wanted to put in the garden next year.

Chapter 7

After school the next evening Danny and Persi went to their homes, ate hurried teas and changed into warm clothes. Two hours later they were back on a bus heading towards Denbury. Robbie had said that if they rang him when they were ready to go home he'd come and pick them up. He'd also given them enough money to buy their bracelets for the evening and have enough over to buy some food and go on the stalls.

As they got off the bus they were met by Neda and Moj and the four of them hurried off to the fairground.

It was noisy, muddy and already crowded when they arrived. They took turns to choose which rides to go on and then Neda and Persi wanted some candy floss while the boys chose hotdogs. Eating these they wandered through the crowds, looking at the stalls and laughing at themselves in the wonky mirrors. As the boys finished their food and started picking at the candy floss they spotted a tent set towards the side of the field, Madam Destiny the sign proclaimed. They read on, 'Let Madam Destiny see into your future, help you find your love, show you how you can find riches.'

"Yeah right, believe that and you'll believe anything!" Moj laughed.

Danny joined in. "Yeah. If she's that good at looking into the future why's she stuck in a place like this?"

As they spoke two girls come out giggling together, followed by Madam Destiny herself. She was dressed in flowing gowns, covered in small mirrors and embroidery showing moon and stars. She was wearing a vivid scarf around her head and her makeup was exotic and showy.

"Ah, young ladies, come in and see what the future holds."

Persi looked up at her quickly, the voice was very familiar. She saw a broad wink on the face that surely couldn't be, yet she knew it was, Rita! She couldn't help smiling at her, but knew that there was no way on earth that she would let the others know her secret.

Neda looked at Persi. "Shall we Persi?"

Danny laughed, "Go on, I'll pay for it."

Persi pulled back. "I'm not sure, I don't think it's a good idea." She looked hard at Rita, hoping for support.

"Come, you're a pretty lady, don't you want to know your future?"

Neda was pulling her into the tent and before she knew it they were both sat in a dim tent, where incense was burning and a crystal ball was sitting on the table.

Rita turned to Neda first. "Give me your hand my darling."

Neda readily gave Rita, or Madam Destiny as she now was, her hand and Rita proceeded to give her some general good news. She then became quite specific about how Neda needed to work hard in her maths classes as she could see that this would be important to her future. Persi knew that Neda liked maths and wondered how on earth Rita could have known this. She realised that Rita was now asking for her hand. She knew that to turn back now would upset Neda and probably Rita and would look suspicious. Reluctantly she gave her hand over. Rita looked closely at it.

"You will be lucky in your endeavours although you will have to travel to dark places to succeed." Well this was no news to her! "I see lots of babies in your hand, not all yours, but you will be very involved with them. You will marry, but not too early, and to someone you don't yet know." Rita looked up at her smiling reassuringly at her. "You will live a long and very happy life and be responsible for many others."

The girls stood up and went out together to meet the boys.

Persi looked around and gave Rita a small wave as they walked away.

"She was very good wasn't she Persi?"

"What? Oh yes, yes very good."

"So what did she say?" the boys both wanted to know.

Neda happily told them that she had to work at her maths and that she was going to have a happy life, and that Persi was going to have lots of babies!

"That's not exactly what she said! She said not all of them were going to be mine." Persi joined in.

She spent the rest of the evening reflecting on what Rita had said. At least she had a future, so whatever happened with the ring, was unlikely to kill her. She felt a great sense of relief at this. She never for a moment considered that Rita might be wrong.

Danny rang his dad and they drove her back to the boat, not going in as it was fairly late and it was a school day the next day, even though it was the one before half term.

Persi went to bed tired and relaxed and slept soundly with no dreams.

Chapter 8

Being half term the next week, she and Neda got together on the Monday to do the project that they had been set for the week. They both felt that it would be good to get it out of the way, and Persi also wanted her mind free in case she heard from her grandma about what Rita might have told her.

Neda had really taken on board the comments about her maths, and she wanted to discuss what Rita might have meant. For a while they tried looking up careers in maths but nothing seemed desperately interesting from their viewpoint. She was interested to know what Persi thought the babies' reference was about. They spent the whole day alternately working, discussing their future and eating a variety of very unhealthy snacks.

The next day Persi's phone rang and she saw it was from her grandma, she answered it excitedly. "Grandma, hi! Have you heard from Rita?"

"Thank you, I'm very well." Grandma laughed, "Nice of you to ask."

"Sorry, I've just been waiting to hear and I guess I sort of forgot everything else."

"Don't worry, I was only teasing. Do you fancy coming over? It would be easier to talk it all through. I thought I'd invite your mum over for tea after she's finished so you can go home together, now the nights are darker."

"Yes that's great. Shall I leave a message on her phone for her? I know she's got appointments for most of the day, and hoped to finish about four."

"That's perfect, see you soon."

Persi locked up the boat and got her bike out. The weather was a bit miserable but not actually raining at that point. By the time she got there she was soaked through. The heavens had opened and she was glad to get into the warmth of her grandma's kitchen.

There was a wonderful vegetable soup and homemade bread ready so she got warm on the inside as well and finally they sat down and Grandma started.

"Well I've heard from Rita, I gather you met her again on Thursday evening?"

"Yes it was a bit of a shock, why didn't you tell me?"

"It didn't occur to me to be honest, and I didn't want you to prejudge her, she really is extremely talented. That's just the way she chooses to live. The fair folk are a lot more accepting of her gifts than most."

"I can imagine, did she say she'd read Neda and my fortunes?"

"No, just that she'd seen you and that you'd recognised her. Did she tell you anything interesting?"

"Lots actually, but it looks as if I'm going to live a long time, which is something of a relief." She laughed, not realising how reassuring she'd found that piece of information.

"I'm very pleased to hear it. Just be aware that she's rarely wrong so you'd be well advised to listen to her."

Persi didn't know if this was a good or a bad thing and thought she'd bring the conversation back.

"So what did she say about the ring?"

"Well as they say, there's good news and there's bad news."

Grandma explained that Rita had said that it was possible for Persi to undertake the quest as she called it. She was to follow quite a few strict rules to do it safely. She'd given Grandma the recipe for a tea that should be drunk just before putting the ring on. It would be bitter but she could add a spoonful or two of grandma's pure honey if she had to. She also had to carry an amulet that she'd instructed grandma to make. And she was only to put the ring on her smallest finger and only when grandma was present. All of this seemed fair enough and not as bad as Persi had imagined. However, the bad news was that she wasn't to do this before the Spring Solstice. That meant towards the end of March.

Persi was distraught. She started to think about the boy, lost in that other world, waiting to be rescued. Also she didn't like to think that he imagined her to be a thief and that he'd been abandoned. She tried to tell this to grandma.

"I know this is a bit of a setback for you, but Rita insists that the time is different in that place, and that it won't make any difference to him. It's hard but she was very definite."

Rita had also instructed Persi to start doing some breathing exercises and meditation, so that she had more control over her mind and body. That was something definite to do and Persi was all up for doing it straight away. She just wasn't quite sure how to do it. Grandma told her that she'd had some thoughts about that.

Eventually the conversation came around to Danny. Grandma asked. "So what are you going to tell Danny about this?"

"The truth, which is that I can't do anything until March, that you'll be alongside me and that I'm going to take all precautions possible." Persi was determined that he should see that she was taking care of herself but that she was going to do it. She felt that if he knew that grandma was going to be there he'd be OK about it.

"Did Rita give any idea about how easy or difficult it might be? Like, you know, how often I might have to go there or anything?" Persi felt that it would be useful to know this sort of thing so that she wouldn't be too despondent if it didn't work our straight away.

"Not directly, but I got the feeling that she thought there would be more than one visit, but I have no idea of the time scale. It's going to depend on you locating the child and then finding the way to get him out."

"I also need to know where to take him, he's not from our time, I don't know if I'm going to have to take him somewhere else. Oh my God, I don't know anything do I? How on earth is this going to work?" Persi began to realise the enormity of the task ahead of her. She desperately wanted to help the boy but thinking about how to do it seemed impossible.

"Come on now, no negative thoughts, you are going to succeed, Rita told you that. Hang onto that thought."

They got up and busied themselves in the kitchen, at least Persi did some preparation and mixing while grandma sat down and got on with some knitting. She'd decided that Robbie and Danny were going to have an Aran jumper each for Christmas and so was getting on with it. Persi suspected that she and her mum were also getting something similar but she saw no evidence while she was there.

Persi was just putting a shepherds' pie in the oven when her mum came in, holding her bag over her head as the rain had started again. "Oh what a day, I'm soaked. Why couldn't it have been a clinic day when the clients came to me, snug inside? Instead I've been in and out of the car most of the day."

Donna, Persi's mum, worked as an aroma therapist and today was obviously not a good day.

Grandma came to the rescue as usual, "Here have a nice hot cup of tea, take your shoes off and sit in front of the Aga."

Once Persi's mum had sat down, warmed up and calmed herself, grandma asked her. "Do you remember that time when you were doing meditation?"

"Oh, gosh, that was a while ago, yes, I can remember really enjoying it. Once we'd moved onto the boat though and I started working and Persi was little, it sort of got lost somehow. I ought to take it up again, it would do me good."

"Just what I wanted to hear. Could you do it alongside Persephone? You know, teach her the basics and practice with her?"

"Yes, if you'd like to Persi?" She looked around at her daughter. Persi nodded vigorously.

"I've still got the tape somewhere, I'll have to see if the player still works." She stopped and looked at her daughter and then at her mother. "OK, what are you two up to?"

Grandma had the decency to look guilty. She explained what Rita had said and how she could help Persi with her 'quest', Persi joined in and told her mum how she knew she had to do it, and wanted her to help.

Attacked from both sides, her mum held her hands in the air and said. "OK.OK. you win. I'm not sure I'm happy about Persi doing this but it looks as if you've thought it all through, so yes, we can do some meditation together, and yes you can do this, but I want it understood that if grandma feels at any time that you should stop, then I will forcibly take the ring from you and throw it in the canal. Is that understood?"

Persi looked at her. "Yes mum, understood."

They settled down to eat the pie and the vegetables that Persi had cooked and agreed that she was becoming as good a cook as her grandma, high praise indeed.

Chapter 9

The next month passed calmly, everything going on much as before, except that Persi and her mum were becoming closer than ever through doing the meditation exercises together. Persi was appreciating the calming effect that it was having and was aware that she could control her thoughts better when she started worrying about how she was going to manage in March.

Having to wait was, if anything, worse than getting straight on with things. She had more time to think about it and imagine all the things that could go wrong.

The dark nights meant that she wasn't seeing as much of Danny and the twins as she had been in the summer, but that was just how it was in the winter months. Danny was working quite a few hours with his dad but Neda had become a trusted friend, although not trusted enough to tell about the ring. Persi wasn't going to make that mistake again. Moj had some boys on the estate that he went around with and life went on quietly. Neda was doing so much better at maths now that it looked as if she'd be going into the next class which meant that they wouldn't be doing that subject together any more but Persi was impressed with her friend's determination. She wished she had got such a clear idea of what she ought to be doing. They still had one evening a week together at grandma's house and Persi sometimes found it hard not to tell Neda about the ring. She still remembered the pain she felt after telling Abby about the necklace and didn't want to put another friendship in jeopardy, so stayed quiet.

Her mum and Robbie were closer than ever and they all spent a lot of time at Robbie's house or at grandma's for Sunday lunch at least once or twice a month.

Suddenly it was Christmas.

They'd decided to spend it at grandma's. She was excited to be cooking a proper Christmas dinner for a family again, and there were enough rooms for them all, with Danny sleeping on the settee.

They all arrived on Christmas Eve and settled in. Typically, the weather was wet and they were glad to curl up in front of the fire. Danny's dog Daisy was in seventh heaven, alternatively lying in front of the fire and then getting up and being fussed by everyone.

They had a leisurely evening and went up to bed looking forward to the following day. Persi dreamt about the boy and the forest but it wasn't such a scary dream as previously so it didn't affect her sleep. She awoke wondering how he was, what he was doing and wondering what he did for food. She shook her head and remembered that she would be going to help him as soon as she could. Then she got dressed quickly and went down to join the others.

Grandma and the two teenagers were down fairly early, well to be fair, Danny had been pushed off the sofa so that they could use it for present opening, and they were waiting for Robbie and Donna to come down. Bacon sandwiches were the breakfast of choice for Danny and Persi, and they were just about finished when a rather flushed Robbie and Donna came down the stairs.

"At last!" Persi cried, "We thought you were never coming down."

"Sorry about that, but we have got a couple of surprises for you!" Robbie replied.

Donna held out her hand and showed off a beautiful solitaire ring. "We're engaged!"

"Oh darling that's wonderful!"

"Wow, you kept that quiet Dad."

"Great news both of you."

All three spoke at once, and everyone laughed and then wanted to see the ring. There were lots of hugs and kisses and a few tears in grandma's eyes.

Disentangling herself, grandma looked up. "You said a couple of surprises." Looking at the two of them.

Donna looked around at Robbie. "Well I wasn't expecting to be proposed to today and Robbie wasn't expecting to be told he was going to be a dad again."

"You're pregnant!"

"A new baby!"

"When?"

The three spoke together again.

Again Donna answered. "Well it's due early summer, a bit before your birthday Persi. Rather earlier than we'd been planning but there you go. I hope everyone's OK with it?"

Robbie chipped in. "I'd hoped we'd get married about then, but we both would like to do it before the baby arrives so we're going to see if we can sort out a wedding in the New Year." He looked at Danny and Persi. "Are you two OK about having a new brother or sister? It's probably a bit of a shock, it was for me, but a good one!" he laughed, but was still looking closely at the two of them.

"Dad it's great, really. Not really that much of a surprise really."

"And I'm really happy about it, we'll be a real family then. Can I be a bridesmaid?" Persi asked, considering this to be the most important aspect.

The rest of the day was taken up with plans for the wedding. Presents were opened. Danny and Robbie loved their jumpers but the heat of the fire stopped them wearing them inside. Donna and Persi had got knitted jackets, not at all what Persi had expected. Hers was a warm chestnut colour with intricate patterns in different shades of bronze running through it, really a work of art, and Donna's was shades of blue, worked in a complicated stitch that looked like basketwork. There was the usual stack of socks, books, chocolates and sweets as well. Robbie and Danny had bought Persi a necklace. It had a silver pendant on it that was a replica of the three swans that started the whole necklace search that summer, and Persi was moved to tears with it. She immediately put it on and everyone was very impressed that they'd found such a suitable present.

In the afternoon the weather cleared so new jumpers and jackets were put on and they enjoyed a walk around the village. In the evening they all played board games until they couldn't keep their eyes open.

"Next Christmas won't be as quiet as this one with a baby around." Mum said as they were going up to bed.

"No, it'll be even better." Robbie smiled at her and looked around at everyone. "We're in for an exciting year I guess."

"We certainly are." Agreed grandma, smiling at Persi. No-one had mentioned her ring or what she was going to do about it but knew that it was at the back of most of their minds, despite the new developments.

The next morning Robbie drove Persi and her mum back to the boat and took Danny home, agreeing that it was the best Christmas ever and that New Year and the wedding were going to be the start of an even better year.

Chapter 10

The wedding was lovely, a quiet affair in the local hotel. Persi was bridesmaid, Danny was best man and it all went off very smoothly. There were several friends from the narrowboats along the canal as well as some of Donna's oldest clients. Grandma baked a cake and put a model boat on it instead of the usual wedding decorations.

Donna moved into the house with Robbie and Danny and after much argument, Persi persuaded everyone that she would spend the week days at Grandma's house and the weekends on the boat. The house had three bedrooms and they would obviously want a room for the baby. Persi reasoned that if they moved the boat off the wharf and bought it into the boat yard, alongside the house, then she could use it as a bedsit, spending the days in the house but sleeping on board.

They'd all been amazed to discover how much stuff Donna had on the boat when it came to moving her into the house and it seemed that most weekends Persi would bring something else to the house that she'd found hidden in a cupboard.

She had downloaded a meditation track onto her tablet and used it at grandma's then her mum joined her on the boat at weekends for them to have some time together. Mum's 'tape' and player were just about finished and Persi teased her about living in the stone age. She was amused to later find that Robbie had bought her mum a CD player and some CD's so the teasing ran out of steam. As her mum got bigger it became harder for her to manage getting on and off the boat and so they moved their sessions into the house, while Robbie and Danny were working in the boatyard.

Persi and Neda spent a lot of time together now and both were keen on getting good grades at school so were often to be found at grandma's house helping each other with different projects. It was quieter there than at Neda's home where the youngsters were always making some sort of noise. In their spare time they would explore the local area as much as the weather would allow. Neda thought that sleeping on the boat was a great treat and so was often found to be staying at the weekends. Persi was enjoying being a teenager with a good friend by her side and although she often thought about the ring, it was not the main thing on her mind.

The warmer weather arrived and suddenly Persi realised that the time had come.

She had thought often about the boy, the forest and how she would solve the mystery, but was training herself to not let it become an obsession.

Spending so much time at grandmas had been lovely. She thought that grandma enjoyed the company and the excuse to cook for someone else! They had discussed the amulet that Rita had told her to make. It had to contain items that would ground Persi to what she knew and loved.

They had started to put things together. A photo of the wedding showing all five of them laughing together, a small embroidered rabbit that had been on Persi's first Babygro; some lavender and mint, her two favourite herbs; a scrap of scarf that still smelt of her mum's favourite perfume; Grandma added a crystal that Rita had suggested, saying it would draw her home. One or two other small items made their way in and grandma used some material from an outgrown but much-loved shirt of Persi's to make a small pouch to put everything in. It wasn't exactly THAT small, but had a cord that held it all together and could be tied around her waist, under her clothes for when she put the ring on.

It was a few days later just after she'd got back to the boatyard from school on a Friday that Persi had a not altogether unexpected phone call from her grandma.

 "Persephone, I've had an interesting phone call from Rita. She's been following your horoscope and says that the next two days would be a good time to try to find your young boy. I'm also to tell you that something unexpected is going to happen but she wasn't clear whether this was to do with the ring or not. It's all a bit confusing to be honest. She said that your way would become clear but not immediately. Anyway would you like to come over tomorrow or Sunday so that we can go into action?"

"Tomorrow would probably be best, I'll get my homework done tonight and with it being Saturday I will have more time, it's nice to be at home on Sundays."

"That's what I thought you'd say. I'll see you back here sometime tomorrow morning then."

Persi took a long time to get to sleep that night, despite doing some meditation and trying to clear her mind, all she could think of was the forest, the boy running away and calling her a thief. She had no idea what might lie ahead of her tomorrow but she was going to do her best.

She told the others that she was going over to see grandma and would be back by tea time but didn't say that this was the day she was going to try again. She decided that they might try to dissuade her or else Danny would insist on coming and she didn't want that sort of pressure on her. She was sure that the steps that she had been taking would be sufficient and knew that Grandma wouldn't let any harm come to her.

Her confidence diminished somewhat as she cycled over. All sorts of negative thoughts kept filling her mind and she arrived breathless and a bit emotional. Grandma took one look at her and made her sit down, drink a cup of camomile tea and talked about what had happened at the WI the other night. They both knew that Persi would remember nothing of the conversation, but it allowed Persi to calm down and the soothing sound of her grandma's voice did more to help her than anything else. She finally put her cup down, looked at her grandma and said. "OK let's do this." She collected her little' bag of luck' as she'd started to call it and tied it to her jeans, tucked under her sweatshirt. She sat on the settee with her grandma alongside and took the ring. She had a cup of the tea that Rita had suggested, with plenty of honey as it was very bitter indeed, and then cautiously she slipped the ring on her little finger as Rita had told her.

Immediately she felt herself falling, further and further down, like Alice in the rabbit hole, but not so pleasant. She came to in the forest again. Whether it was the same part or not she couldn't tell. She remembered the gloom but this time her eyes adjusted more easily, possibly because they knew there was light there. There was still the musty, rather unpleasant smell and she felt the undefined threat that seemed to run throughout the whole place.

She looked around, hoping to see some sort of sign. Which way should she go and what should she do when she got there? There was a rustling in the undergrowth behind her and she turned quickly. She felt that she was being watched but could see nothing. She decided that it would be better to go toward her fears rather than run from them, so she walked towards the trees where the sound had come from.

"Don't come any closer." It was the boy, she recognised his voice. "How did you do that?"

"Do what?"

"You know, disappear and then come back like that."

"I don't know what you mean." Persi couldn't understand what he meant, it was months since she'd been here before. He was speaking as if it was all done in a moment.

"One minute you were here, and then you disappeared and a few moments later, you were here again."

She walked towards the voice as she tried to reply, without frightening him again. "Will you tell me your name?"

"I'm Willem, but you know that don't you?" He sounded angry again, and Persi was scared that he'd run off again and she knew that she couldn't catch up with him.

"Willem, that's a nice name, but I really don't know who you are. No-one's sent me, but I'd like to try to take you home. I just don't know how to do it at the moment. Could you help me, tell me more about yourself and your mother?"

She heard a sob. Slowly he emerged from the bushes just in front of her. She couldn't believe that she hadn't seen him, he was only feet away.

"How do you have my mother's ring? I don't understand. I'm so tired and I just want to go home."

"Of course you do, come here." She held out her arms and to her surprise he ran into them and hugged her. Poor little thing, she thought. He was so small and fragile, how had he survived in this awful place.

"Now listen, this isn't going to make much sense to you and I don't understand much of it myself, but maybe together we can work out what to do. Your mother's ring was on sale at a market and I bought it. I put it on and it bought me here. Then when I took the ring off, I went back to my home. I've put it on again and now I'm back here. Tell me, how long do you think you have been here?"

"I don't know, lots of days I think, probably a week or two." DAYS Persi thought! He'd been here for months to her knowledge and heaven knows how long it might have been before that. What was this place? She felt him tense.

"She's coming, quick hide, she mustn't see us." He pulled her down into the bushes and expertly pulled some over them. He put a dirty hand over her mouth and looked straight into her eyes. The message was clear. She stayed as still and as silent as she could and felt a chill pass across her, as if someone had opened a fridge door and let all the cold air out. The feeling gradually passed and slowly Willem took his hand away but still cautioned her to be quiet with his eyes.

Minutes passed and finally he breathed a deep sigh and said. "She's gone for now. I think that she knows you're here. But for some reason she can't find you. You have to hope that she doesn't."

"Who is she and what does she do?"

"She is evil. She tells you things that make you feel sad and worthless. She keeps creatures tied up on ropes and makes them fight each other. I've heard their cries. She can take your heart from your body, at least that's what it feels like. When I first saw you I thought that you were here at her orders to capture me. She knows I'm here, and she has sent thoughts to me, but never captured me. I'm too quick and I know how to hide."

"You certainly do. What can you tell me about your mother? Is she here too?"

"No. Mother is at home I expect, wondering what has happened to me. I was out in the woods one day trying to catch a rabbit and I tripped over something. The next thing I knew I was here. I can remember hearing my mother calling to me just before it happened and then nothing."

"What was your mother's name and where did you live, can you remember?"

"We live in a small wagon and travel around for my father to mend pots and pans and do work for people. We were last at a place called Eyam, it's high up on the moors, my mother's name is Hilde. My father died of a sickness. Many were sick I remember."

This meant nothing to Persi, but it was clear that he was not talking about her time. It sounded like a long time ago and she realised that his words were not said in the way she knew but that she could understand them, in the same way that she could understand the Vikings in her previous dreams. His language was closer to the one that

Gunnar's wife had spoken. Was he from the same time? Persi felt completely confused.

She looked down to him. "Willem, I'm going to have to go to try to find where your mother might be. I don't know Eyam but I'm going to find out. You have to believe that I will come back but now I have to go. I'll be back soon."

"No, no don't leave me...." She heard his cries but she also heard her mother calling her, urgently. She took the ring off, with no problem this time and found herself back at grandma's. She looked around.

"Where's mum?"

"Why she's at home, she's not been here. What happened this time?"

"I have to go. I'll be in touch but I feel something strong about mum. I've got to get to her, she needs me."

Persi ran out of the house, grabbed her cycle and left without even giving Grandma a goodbye kiss, she'd even left her jacket behind.

Chapter 11

She had never cycled so fast along the tow path in all her life and was glad that there weren't any walkers out today to slow her down. Her mum was crying. What on earth was wrong?

She arrived back at the boatyard and immediately ran to their boat, rather than the house. She climbed in and to her horror saw her mum lying on the floor in a pool of clear liquid.

"The baby's coming Persi and it's too early. I haven't got my phone and ahhh." She stopped talking to grab hold of her belly and groan.

"Don't worry mum, I'm here, we'll get you sorted out." Persi ran to her mum's old bedroom and pulled the covers off the bed, found some towels and put them on it and went back to her. "Right we're going to get you up onto the bed and then I'll try to get some help." Her mum grabbed Persi's hand. "Don't leave me Persi, I can't do this."

"Yes you can and of course I won't leave you." Persi reassured her whilst supporting her between contractions to get through to the bed. She lay down looking exhausted.

"Mum, I just want to feel your tummy, is that OK?"

"Mmmm." She groaned as another contraction came. Persi rested her hands on her mum's stomach and immediately felt the tension in her body. As she kept my hands there, the muscles relaxed and she became calm again. Persi concentrated all her energies into what was happening inside her mum and realised that the baby was nearly here.

"Mum I really need to try to get some help, I'll just pop outside and see if I can call Robbie or Danny."

"You can't, they've gone off to look at a boat that's broken down a couple of miles away."

"Then I shall ring 999" Luckily she got a signal in the boat, for a change, and quickly alerted the emergency services, then turned back to her mum. She'd been able to do most of that with one hand still on the tummy and although she had had some pains, they didn't appear to be so intense. Then there was a change. She could feel it coming through her fingers right into her own body, the baby was determined to come.

She got her mum as comfortable as possible as she suddenly gave a huge push and there was the top of a head appearing. "It's nearly here mum. You're doing really well." Another push and it was out! She couldn't believe it, a new baby brother was already screaming blue murder. She ran to the kitchen and grabbed some kitchen twine and a knife, hoping they were clean enough and instinctively tied off the cord and cut it, handing the new boy to mum. They were both in tears as Persi found another towel to wrap him in.

In the distance they could hear the ambulance but knew that it couldn't go too fast along the winding lanes. Persi was aware of mum's body pushing again and so she grabbed the washing up bowl as she'd read somewhere that it was important to know that the whole placenta was there. As it emerged, she realised that it wasn't the placenta, it was another baby, far smaller but this one was blue and didn't cry immediately. She looked at mum, but she was so busy sorting herself out to get the baby to start his first feed that she hadn't seen her daughters' distress.

Persi took the tiny doll like form and held it in her hands, she was that small. She bent down and breathed across her face rubbing her chest with her finger. Suddenly she moved, a slight movement it was true but nonetheless, there was life. The baby started to turn a better colour and gave out a gentle mew. Persi broke into tears and wrapped the little girl in another towel. "Mum, mum, here, you have a little girl as well, they were twins."

Her mum looked up in shock, the boy was greedily feeding and her attention was on him. The second baby didn't seem real to her. Not that is until Persi held her out and both babies were curled up on her chest.

"How on earth did they miss her? The scan only showed one baby. I can't believe this." And she promptly burst into tears. This was the scene that the ambulance staff, followed shortly by grandma, met with when they got on the boat. The paramedics checked the three of them over and said that as both babies were so early, they would need to get to the Special Care Unit and they were very concerned with the health of the little girl, as she was obviously struggling.

Grandma had left the boat with Persi while the examinations were going on and was listening to Persi's account of the proceedings. As the mother and babies were carefully taken out of the boat to be transferred into the ambulance, grandma asked her daughter. "What are you going to call them?" "George, after dad, we'd already decided on that, but I don't know about the little girl." "Hope, you must call her Hope." Said Persi, without even thinking about it. Donna smiled up at her and replied, "That's beautiful Persi, Hope she shall be."

With that the ambulance driver shut the doors and took them off. Grandma and Persi looked at one another. "We'd best ring Robbie I think and tell him the good news!"

"Heavens yes, I can't believe I didn't think of that."

"I think you've probably had enough to be thinking about in the last hour or so." Grandma laughed and pulled her into a hug, where both of them found themselves laughing and crying at the same time.

Later that night she had to tell the story again to a rather frazzled looking Robbie and an admiring Danny. "How did you know to come over? You were at grandmas' weren't you?" asked Robbie. Persi looked guiltily at Grandma who was strangely looking in the other direction.

"I was going back with the ring and suddenly I heard mum crying for me. I just took the ring off, came back to grandma's, cycled like crazy and got here in time."

Robbie looked at her in admiration, Danny's look was less happy. Robbie spoke. "Well thank goodness for your intuition or whatever it is Persi, I for one will be forever in your debt. Heaven knows what would have happened with George and Hope if you hadn't been there."

Grandma interrupted. "Let's just be grateful that she WAS there. Now then, when did they say they'd be home?"

Diversion tactics but they worked. Robbie explained that he'd go in to see them again in the morning and see how they were. Hope wouldn't be able to come home for a while but George seemed to be doing fine. It turned out that they were due a bit earlier than they had originally thought so the babies weren't as premature as expected.

"Do you mind me naming Hope, Danny. It just came out, I didn't mean to take over or anything." Persi had been worrying how Robbie felt at finding that not only had he got an unexpected new daughter but that she came with a name already.

"Hope is perfect for her, and if anyone had a right to name her then you did." He smiled warmly at her and she was relieved, it had been worrying her a bit.

Grandma and Persi had spent some time cleaning up the boat while waiting for Robbie and Danny to get back from the hospital and so it was decided that they would both sleep there that night and all go in to see the new family in the morning.

Chapter 12

After a hearty breakfast they went in to visit. Persi was amazed to see her mum looking positively glowing and busily feeding George when they arrived. She looked around but there was no sign of Hope.

"It's all right Persi, Hope is fine, just a bit small so she's in an incubator down the hall. You can go and see her if you like."

Persi went off in search of her new sister. A nurse showed her the little girl in the incubator with various tubes attached to her. She looked so much smaller and more vulnerable than she had yesterday. The nurse noticed her expression. "Don't worry, she's doing fine. This is just so that we can ensure that she's kept in the best conditions so that she'll soon be able to join her brother." Persi watched Hope as she opened her eyes and appeared to look straight at her. She knew it was impossible but she felt a very strong bond with this baby. George was going to be able to look after himself, she reckoned, but this one will need me to watch over her. She smiled at Hope and the baby blinked and then shut her eyes, seemingly content.

Persi went back to her mother's room. "She's so small and yet so perfect. Do you know when they will let her out?"

"Nothing definite, but I'm going to stay here with George for a couple of days so that she can easily have my milk and then we'll see how we get on."

Grandma took over from here. "Right then, I'll see that they are all fed and watered at home and get some things sorted out so that both the babies have a bed to come home to. I've already had offers of lots of bits of equipment from my ladies in the village and you don't need to worry about a thing. When you come home, I'll stay on the boat with Persi and help out so that Robbie can get some work done. There's an end to it."

They all looked at her and each other then said a united. "Thank you."

Grandma took Persi and Danny down to the cafeteria for a drink and a biscuit to allow the new parents some time together.

"You don't need to worry about food and all that, we'll look after ourselves grandma." Danny spoke once he'd finished the biscuit.

"I know you can do it, but now I've said that, Donna will have nothing to worry about apart from herself and those babies. It's not a good idea for Persi to be over at my house when either of us might be needed at any time so it makes sense for me to stay on the boat, as long as Persi doesn't mind that is?"

"Of course not, you're always welcome, you know that."

"Right well in that case, I think I'd better get you two back home so that we can start sorting out this nursery." Danny texted his dad to say that they were going back in grandma's car so he could stay as long as he liked.

Once home they started sorting out the room that had been designated the nursery. Robbie and Donna had started putting things in there but it was far from sorted. Grandma spent some time ringing around her friends and soon cars started to arrive with a second cot, bags of baby clothes, changing mats and all the other paraphernalia that babies apparently needed to have. One person even turned up with a double pram that they were no longer using and after some negotiation, grandma proudly wheeled it into the house.

Robbie had texted to say that he'd stay with the others through the day but would be home early evening. That meant that by the time he came home they were all totally exhausted but the nursery was now ready for use. For once in her life Grandma was happy to have a take-away as none of them had done more than drink tea and eat odd pieces of cake or biscuits that were found in the larder.

Robbie came home with the news that he'd had a cuddle with Hope, she was now feeding properly and they just wanted to observe her for a couple more days and as long as she had gained a bit of weight she could come home. Donna had therefore decided to stay there until she could bring both babies home.

As they sat around late that evening, all of them too wound up to go to bed, but all of them exhausted Danny finally turned to Persi and asked her how her trip with the ring had gone.

Slowly, trying to remember all the details, she related everything she could about Willem and all he had said. When she mentioned Eyam, Robbie interrupted her. "The plague village?"

"What? Sorry do you know it?" Persi was surprised.

"Yes of course, it's not far from here, up in the Peak District. It's very famous." Grandma nodded but didn't interrupt. "When the plague came up to this area, this one village barricaded themselves in as soon as they realised that they had it there. People from the surrounding villages would come and leave supplies at the boundaries and by doing this they contained the plague in a small place and saved countless lives."

"That fits with what Willem told me, he said his father had died and lots of people were ill, he was out looking for food when he says he fell over and found himself in the forest he's trapped in. I think I need to go there and get a feel for the place, it might help me know what to do with him and how to help him."

"I'd take you, but with the babies and the boatyard, I'm a bit stretched at the moment." Robbie looked about to fall asleep.

"I'll take them next weekend, but come on you two, it's school tomorrow and you need some sleep, it's been a long weekend."

No-one was about to argue with this and in very little time each of them were tucked up in their own beds, with their own dreams.

Chapter 13

The next week passed quickly, mother and babies all came home on Thursday, as they'd had to wait for Hope to put on a couple more ounces, something she'd done quite easily once she'd discovered the delights of feeding. Persi had gone to see them all and spent most of the time holding her new sister and it seemed that Hope gained strength from her. She was always going to be smaller than George, but everyone could see a determination in her not to be left behind. George was calm and placid and as long as he was fed and clean, he was happy to sleep. Hope seemed to think that if she slept she was missing something and so already their characters were forming.

On Saturday, there were plenty of Donna's friends willing to come and help while grandma took Persi and Danny to Eyam. It was a pleasant day, just at the end of March and the bluebells were showing through the woodlands as they drove up into the Peak District. Eyam immediately felt special to Persi. She had bought her' bag of luck' and the ring with her and as they wandered around the houses that still remained from that terrible time. Persi noted that the year was 1665 when the tragedy struck and realised that Willem had been in that awful forest for over 350 years. And he had described it as days, possibly a couple of weeks. What was she to do?

They went into the churchyard but there was no reaction. Persi had hoped that she'd feel some connection there.

They discovered the museum, a delightful old building at one end of the village. Going in they discovered the names and houses of those who had died and those who had survived, but there was no mention of a Hilde. Then Persi remembered that Willem had said that they were travelling through, so of COURSE there would be no record of them.

They also discovered that because so many had died in such a short time they had buried their dead in their gardens rather than get together in a group at the church. Apparently they realised that they were more at risk when lots of people were together, so they tried to avoid this as much as possible. That would explain why there was no connection in the churchyard.

They went back out and grandma went back to sit in the car, near the church while Persi and Danny went off up the hill past the museum. They went into the car park where they could see the landscape and suddenly Persi felt the ring pulling her.

"It's around here somewhere, this is where they were staying." It seemed logical, there was a water source nearby and it would be close to the village, without being in anyone's way.

They hurried back to the car and told grandma what they had discovered.

"I know how much you want to help this young boy, but we must think this through. It's not a set of necklaces you want to unite this time, it's a person. Someone who has been dead for a long time but still lingers on in a dark and dangerous place. I think I need to talk to Rita again. I'm sorry Persi but I haven't got any answers for you this time."

Persi went over and hugged her, feeling sad for both of them and grateful that Danny hadn't said anything, she knew he didn't want her to do this but he just sent a weak smile her way and looked off into the distance.

On the way home they all tried to come up with solutions to the problem, some helpful, some hilarious and Persi was glad to be able to laugh about it. She realised that she hadn't done any meditation for the last week and determined to start again when she got home. She knew that whatever happened she'd need to have the inner strength that meditation gave her to cope with it. Maybe she could get her mum back to it, if she had five minutes' break from the twins at any time.

Chapter 13

With all the fuss about the babies and the visit to Eyam, Persi had forgotten that the Easter holidays were upon them. She also realised that she'd been forgetting Neda in all the fuss so she invited her over to the boat and for a peek at the babies. Grandma had gone home after the first week once she'd got Robbie to solemnly swear that he'd ring her if there was any need, and she'd be over. Persi had stayed to help out and ensure that her mum wasn't doing too much, also to cuddle Hope at any opportunity.

Neda was suitably impressed with them and told Persi that she was now a bit of a celebrity in the area. The local press had heard about "Teenager delivers own brother and sister – saves their lives" heaven only knows where they got it all from but they had a photo of Donna and the twins in hospital and one of Persi's recent school photos.

"Oh for goodness sake, I had no idea, where did they get all of this?" Persi asked, rather exasperated.

Neda told her that she'd heard from someone who knew someone, that one of the other patients on the ward was a relation of the reporter and the photo had been taken by one of the cleaners, they'd done it to give Robbie but had conveniently forgotten to mention that they'd given a copy to the press. It was all highly illegal Persi felt and was upset that her name was being used like that. She liked her privacy.

Much to her surprise, Abby came over as well and gave the twins a present from her mother and spent some time with Persi on the boat. It was rather uncomfortable at first but Abby said she was "Well impressed." With Persi and what she'd done and wanted the gory details, which Persi wasn't going to tell her. She left after a bit and Persi knew that she wouldn't be seeing her again except at school. Neda was completely different. She respected Persi's privacy and hadn't asked anything apart from whether Persi had been frightened and how she'd known what to do.

Persi was tempted to tell her about her ability to calm and heal. She remembered the incident with Abby's horse, Panda and mending Danny's injuries and then realised how her touch had calmed her mother. She decided against it though, maybe one day but not now.

The weather was improving steadily and she and Neda took the twins out for a walk once or twice during the days to give her mum time to rest.

All the time though, at the back of Persi's mind was what was she going to do about Willem?

She'd tried sitting down with Danny and asking him for any help, but he'd not been able to think of anything that could be done. He was also still very worried about Persi getting drawn into something that would hurt her. She ended up telling him all about Rita and Madame Destiny and after that he felt a bit more relaxed about Persi's dilemma. That is after he stopped laughing about Persi and having her fortune told at the fair. They realised that Rita had told Persi that she'd have babies in her hands that weren't hers and Persi also remembered that Rita had predicted that there would be something unexpected the day that the babies were born but up till then she hadn't made the connection. Remembering all of this helped Persi relax a bit more as well and she and Danny slipped back into their old easy ways that neither of them had realised had changed since she first put the ring on.

Chapter 14

During the second week of the holidays, grandma rang up to say that she'd spoken to Rita and would Persi like to go over for the next day? She checked with her mum, who said that was fine. Grandma had filled the freezer with meals, Persi had cleaned the house over the last few days and she had Robbie and Danny in the boatyard on the end of a phone if she needed them. She'd been able to have a few words with Danny before she went and he'd wished her good luck and said that if she needed him, she only had to ask and he'd be there for her.

Persi got her bike out and cycled along the towpath. There were a few boats moving now and she realised that life was going on and felt more relaxed and at ease than she'd done for a while. She'd been keeping up her meditation and hardly needed the CD now. In fact, all was well with her world.

She arrived at Grandma's therefore in a very positive mood. She found her out in the garden, looking over her early salad crops. "Ah, there you are Persephone, good it must be time for a cup of something!"

They went inside and after Persi had told Grandma all the latest about the babies she asked what was going to happen next about the ring.

"Well I've spoken to Rita and basically she's said to trust your instinct, as long as you do all that she'd told you to do so far."

This news took Persi by surprise, she thought that there would be a new set of instructions and tasks to do, so this was a shock.

"Right, in that case, let's look at what we know. First there is Willem, who must have died when out hunting for food." Grandma nodded, but didn't interrupt.

"Then we know where his family were, and that they probably died in the same place by the wagon, where I felt the ring calling."

Another nod.

"Then all I have to do it to get Willem and take him back there so he can be with his family."

"That's all there is to it Persephone. Have you any ideas as to how to go about it?" Grandma gave

Persi a reassuring smile, quite impressed that Persi had it all so clearly organised.

"Well, I've been giving it some thought, but expected Rita to have some objections, but if I can do it my way, then we will go back to Eyam and go to the car-park. Then I'll put the ring on and hope to get back to the place where I left Willem, and then I thought that if I held onto him while using the ring I'd come back and he'd sort of, well I don't know, be released, I suppose."

"And what of the ring?"

"What do you mean?"

"If the ring wants to reunite Willem with his mother shouldn't you leave it with him?"

"You mean give it to him? I'm not sure how that would work, if I take it off it brings me straight back, how can I give it to him and know that he'll be OK?"

"Maybe you need to just trust your judgement on that one, but give it some thought in the meantime. Shall we go up to Eyam this weekend before you start back at school?"
"Do you mind? I'd like to get it sorted out if possible, it seems to have been around for ever.

Such a lot has happened to me since I found the ring, and I worry about that poor boy, wandering around that awful place."

"Stop worrying, that's not going to help anyone. Right, enough about the ring, lets sort out some lunch."

Chapter 16

Persi told Danny what she'd planned to do and he insisted that he come along as well. It became a family conference over dinner and it was agreed that it would be best if Danny went along, for moral support. Persi was pleased in one way but worried that him worrying about her would make it harder. As it turned out it was very lucky he went.

Saturday dawned wet and windy. Grandma turned up as planned to pick the two of them up and after a short cuddle with the twins and a chat to see that her daughter was all right, grandma, Persi and Danny set off.

As they got into the peaks, the weather worsened and as they wound up the hill and rounded the corner to take them into the village, the sky seemed to be throwing rain down on them.

They pulled into the car-park and were not surprised to find that they were the only ones there.

Grandma had bought the tea for Persi that Rita had recommended in a flask and put plenty of honey in it to make it taste a bit better. Persi drank it with a slight shudder and checked that her lucky pouch was firmly attached to her jeans and tried to clear her mind with a few deep breaths.

"I know it's horrible out there but I feel I ought to be outside, staying in the car isn't an option I'm afraid, but you two can stay here."

"Don't be daft, there's no way I'm letting you out there on your own."

"Exactly, Danny's right, I've got a brolly and we'll be fine, don't you worry about us, you just get on with what you need to do and we'll sort ourselves out."

Persi climbed out of the car into the rain. She was wet immediately and suddenly wondered what on earth she was doing. Shaking herself inwardly she felt inside her anorak to reassure herself that her lucky bag was there and then untied it from her jeans and put it into her pocket so that she could stay in touch with it. Turning towards the others getting out of the car she smiled weakly at them and hesitantly put the ring onto her little finger.

As expected she immediately found herself back in the forest. Was it her imagination or did it seem even more threatening than usual? She looked around hoping to spot Willem, but there was no sign of him this time. Should she call out to him? Worried that any loud noise might bring more than the boy to her she looked around to see if there was any discernible path. She thought that she could make out a faint track and so she started out along it, trusting to her instinct to take the right path.

She hadn't gone far when she thought she heard a cry off to her left. Part of her was worried that it meant that Willem was in trouble and the other part hoped it meant that she was close to him. Turning she pushed her way through the undergrowth and only went a few feet before she heard another cry, this time it sounded as if it was on her right, so she turned again. The undergrowth seemed to be conspiring against her and she was getting more tangled up in the brambles when she heard another cry, much louder this time and behind her.

Then she heard the voice again. It was the same voice that she'd heard the first time she was here.

"You again, I told you that you couldn't get out of here." This was followed by laughter, the same nasty laughter as before.

This time Persi decided that it wasn't worth answering. She turned away and ignored the cries that continued to try to lure her from all angles. Once again Persi found the brambles catching her but she was rather more careful to avoid the stinging nettles this time.

She refused to hurry but hoped that just by walking through the forest calmly would mean that Willem could find her.

The forest appeared to have no recognisable landmarks, it was just trees, surrounded by more trees and then yet more. Persi thought a few times that she recognised something only to realise that it wasn't anything special. There were certainly ups and downs and once again she found herself going downwards towards the sound of water. This filled her with hope, she was sure that she'd met Willem near water.

Suddenly there was another familiar voice. "You again, I told you not to come here, this place is mine. Go or I'll summon her." A pause then a horrible yell that started deep inside and became higher and higher as it went on. It echoed around the trees and filled Persi with terror. Forgetting what happened the last time she ran unseeing in this awful place, she turned and ran.

Her breath was coming in short pants and she felt tears streaming down her face. Suddenly she felt a chill. Too late she remembered that Willem had hid her when this had happened before and before she knew what was happening she looked up to see an apparition in front of her.

There was a shape, humanlike but much taller. It seemed to be female but made more of a grey swirling mist rather than flesh and blood. The eyes, or in the place where the eyes would be, there were dark red circles and the hole that would have been the mouth was open wide and emitting an awful mocking laugh.

Persi told herself that she could leave at any time and that none of this was real. She also put her hand in her pocket and held the bag tightly. Trying not to show how scared she felt, she stood up as high as she could and demanded in as clear a voice as she could muster, and said.

"You don't scare me. What are you doing?"

Stupid thing to say she thought to herself, but it was too late to think up anything more intelligent on the spur of the moment.

"You are in my kingdom now little girl, you will be one of my toys. You look as if you could be quite amusing."

Persi thought back to what Willem had told her. Was this the 'queen' that he'd spoken about and who he had been hiding from all this time? If so, then she hadn't done much to help him had she?

She thought of taking her ring off now and getting away but the very realisation that she could do this gave her courage.

"I don't think that you'd find me much fun after a while, I'm not interested in you and I think I shall leave now."

There was a horrible laughing sound that seemed to be coming from the shape in front of her.

"Oh but you are showing yourself to be great fun! No-one had tried to defy me for a long time, I think you'll be a real asset to my collection."

Without warning Persi felt herself bound by cords that appeared from no-where, and she was being escorted through the undergrowth which was moving and allowing her a clear path.

Chapter 17

In no time at all, Persi found herself in a clearing with several young children standing around, taking no notice of her. Looking at them they appeared to have stepped straight out of an illustrated history book. None were apparently as old as her but they were of different ethnic origins and their clothes showed that some of them must have been here for many hundreds of years.

They all appeared lifeless and still no-one looked at her or seemed interested in her arrival.

She went up to the girl who was nearest to her.

"Hello, I'm Persi, what's your name?"

The child didn't appear to notice her and continued gazing into space.

Looking around she realised that none of them were talking or taking any notice of each other or trying to amuse themselves. They were just there.

The silence wasn't total though, she could hear the forest sounds around her, all quite distant, nothing seemed close to her somehow. It was as if she was in a bubble and everything else was outside and slightly muffled.

She went towards a tree and sat down leaning her back against it. The cords had disappeared and she realised that she was free but she had a feeling that if she tried to leave the clearing she'd not be able to do so.

She turned the ring on her finger with her thumb but for some reason didn't want to take it off at the moment. She thought back and remembered that Rita had told her to trust her instincts, and at the moment it was to stay here.

Since she was no longer tied up, she tried walking around. Nothing happened which rather surprised her. Then she started to walk towards the edge of the clearing and she found that her legs seemed to be heavy. It was rather like trying to walk when she was in the swimming pool. Possible but slow and unsteady. The further from the centre of the clearing she went the harder it was to move until she found herself at a standstill, unable to more forward any further. She turned and found that walking back into the clearing was fine. She was obviously a prisoner here. 'No' she thought, 'I'm NOT a prisoner, I can leave here whenever I want.'

Suddenly the chill that she had felt earlier surrounded her and the apparition was back. "You've discovered some of my powers have you?" then there was more laughter. Did everyone have to laugh in this awful place, thought Persi. She was getting irritated at the stupidity of the situation, as well as being more scared than she wanted to admit.

"I have powers." She stated, surprising herself by how determined she sounded.

"You? You have powers! A child like you cannot imagine the powers I have."

"Oh but I can. Your powers are all bad and for yourself, but mine are stronger because I can heal and help people and I think that is better." As she spoke she started to believe in herself. She could hear Rita telling her she had a long life and her great-grandmother telling her how special she was and how great her powers would be. She was filled with a real anger against this, this puff of wind that she saw in front of her.

The laughter stopped and the chill became colder. She started shivering and could hear her teeth begin chattering. Thrusting her hand into her pocket she felt her 'bag of luck' and the chill faded, she smiled at the thing in front of her and walked across to the child nearest her. She laid her hands on the almost frozen form and took a deep breath and concentrated all her thoughts on it. To her horror the child looked at her, smiled and then turned to dust in front of her.

"NO, that was mine. You cannot take my toys from me."

The chill threatened to engulf Persi again, but again she breathed deeply and reached inside herself for her own personal strength and moved to the next child. She repeated her hands on experiment, and was not surprised this time when the child became dust.

The screams coming from the apparition were ear-splitting now and seemed to fill the whole forest but Persi continued to walk around and release the children from whatever had held them. When finally the last child had gone and there was only Persi and the apparition left in the clearing, she was so calm and so much in control that she felt that anything was possible.

Looking at the apparition she calmly took the ring from her finger and ….. found herself still in the clearing with the screaming, ice cold apparition in front of her.

Chapter 18

Meanwhile in the car park, Danny was getting more and more concerned about Persi, she had gone stone cold and he was finding it hard to find a pulse. He found that she'd already taken the ring off and it was just held in her other hand, but it didn't seem to have the usual effect. This really worried him but he didn't want to tell grandma as she didn't seem to be coping that well with Persi's predicament.

Grandma kept saying, "Rita has seen her future, she'll be all right." Like a mantra, over and over again. Usually so calm and in control, she looked suddenly much older than her 60 something years.

Danny took control. "We must get her into the car, and get her warm. Somethings gone wrong. Can you get her legs if I take her shoulders?"

Pulling herself together, Persi's grandma took her feet and with some difficulty they got her in the car. They were all wet through as they'd had to put the umbrellas down while getting Persi in the car and Danny asked grandma to turn the engine on and get the heating going. In the meantime, he looked in the boot and found an old picnic blanket that he wrapped around Persi.

"Is there any more of that tea in your thermos?" he asked.

"Yes, but I'm not sure if it will still be all that hot."

"I don't think we need to worry about that. We've just got to get her warm."

Danny forced the bitter liquid into Persi's mouth and was glad to feel the heater start to warm the air.

"Perse, Perse, come on girl, come back to us. Think of Hope, she needs her big sister to look out for her, come on, please, please Perse."

Grandma had climbed into the back and they had sat Persi up between them hoping that the combined body heat would get through to her.

It seemed a long time but they realised that rather than feeling as if a block of ice was sat between them, there was some warmth. That renewed their efforts and they took a hand each and kept rubbing it between their own hands.

There was a murmur, "Hope, Hope I'm here, I'm here." Then Persi put her head on Danny's shoulder and seemed to go to sleep. Her temperature started to return to normal and Danny could feel a strong pulse again. He and grandma exchanged a relieved look and then she spoke.

"I think she'll be OK now Danny. Can you help me put her seat belt on and I think we'd better get her home and into bed." Grandma sounded very old all of a sudden and Danny looked at her wondering if she was going to be all right. She caught his look and smiled weakly at him.

"I'm so pleased you came with us Danny. I don't know how I'd have managed on my own."

"Never mind that now, let's just get back if you feel up to driving?"

"Oh don't you worry about me, I've just had a bit of a shock, well we both have, once I get going I'll be fine. Are you OK back there with her?"

Danny nodded and smiled at her in the rear view mirror and they started for home.

The drive home was uneventful and grandma just concentrated on driving whilst checking the two teenagers in the back in the mirror every so often.

When they got back to the boatyard, Danny ran in and found his dad. Robbie was very worried when he was asked to carry Persi into the house but the others promised to tell everything once Persi was inside.

Luckily her mum was out with the babies and they were able to settle Persi in Danny's room. She hadn't woken or said anything else since she'd come too, but her colour was healthy and she was breathing evenly so they were relatively happy with her.

By the time Donna and the twins came back the others had explained what had happened to Robbie. Then they had to go through it again for Donna. They had a meal although no-one ate much and they took it in turns to pop up to check that Persi was OK.

Donna went up later in the evening with Hope in her arms. She went into Danny's room, pulled back the covers a bit and put Hope in next to Persi, then she sat on the bed watching her two daughters sleeping. One with honey coloured skin, very dark hair with red hints and long black eyelashes resting on her cheeks. The other like a little rosebud in comparison, a slight blond downy growth on her head and light brown eyelashes.

Both so precious. Persi stirred, feeling the warmth of the little body next to her. She opened her eyes and looked down. "Hello Hope, I was dreaming about you." And she dropped a kiss on the baby's head.

She looked up. "Hi mum, what's going on, what are you doing here?" she looked around. "And why am I in Danny's bedroom?"

Donna laughed. "Welcome home my beautiful girl. We'll tell you all about it later."

Chapter 19

A bit later that evening Persi was downstairs filling up on a big bowl of soup and a chunk of bread. The others were joining her, since they hadn't eaten much at tea.

Persi listened to Danny's account of what had happened to her.

Slowly she took a deep breath and seemed to be thinking hard.

"I didn't find Willem but I think I know what the place is where he's trapped." She looked around and could see the concern in their eyes, but knew that she had to make them understand. "I believe that Willem had the plague and died when he was in the forest. For some reason he didn't die properly and his soul was left in a sort of underworld, I don't know how to explain it, but he's trapped, not able to rest. I think that forest is in his imagination and it's all the things he hated most. It's really not a nice place." She breathed again and was grateful that no-one had interrupted her, not realising that they had made a pact to let her talk it through before they asked her anything.

"There are, no there WERE, other children who I think were also there, I don't know how that worked but I was able to release them, I got them out of there. It was amazing, scary but amazing. I had more power than her. She tried to freeze me, to entrap me, but I came back, I don't know how. I took the ring off but I didn't come back then." At that point she burst into tears.

Her mum put her arms around her and rocked her like a baby. When she was calmer, she asked Persi. "Would you like to have grandma tell you what happened?"

"Mmm, I think so." She smiled wanly.

Grandma told her how she had gone cold but that she Danny had bought her around and that it was when Danny mentioned Hope that she was properly back and that she had fallen asleep. They had worked out what to say while she was asleep. They didn't want to scare her too much and they didn't want to mention the ring until Persi asked about it.

Strangely Persi didn't mention it. She could remember taking it off and then not coming back but hadn't as yet thought about what had happened to it. The rest felt that the longer it was before she asked about it, the better.

It was agreed that Persi and grandma would sleep in the boat that night, after Persi had point blank refused to stay in Danny's bed. She swore that if she woke up to see some of the Star Wars posters looking down at her in the night she'd never sleep again.

She pointed out that if grandma was with her she'd be fine and that they were only a few steps away from the house in any case if there was any need for help.

Surprisingly Persi slept soundly that night, with no bad dreams. She was the only one, grandma in the next room and the three in the house all spent a restless night, worrying about what was going to happen next, because no-one believed that this was the end of Persi's search to free Willem.

Chapter 20

The next morning, a Sunday, there was a very subdued breakfast before grandma drove herself back home after checking that the family were still coming over for a roast later that day.

Persi was aware that everyone else was in a nervous state and felt that she was the cause, but couldn't cope with discussing it yet. To avoid that she put the twins in their pram and went for a walk. Danny asked if he could tag along and she reluctantly agreed. She'd really have liked to be on her own but got the impression that Danny wanted to keep his eyes on her. This put her in a defensive mood and it was one of the most uncomfortable times they had spent together since they had become friends again the previous year.

"I don't need a minder you know. I'm quite safe with them."

"Don't be stupid, I know you're perfectly all right on your own. I just…I want…Look I was really scared yesterday. I, well, I thought you were dead. I didn't know how I was going to come home and explain to our dad and mum that you were dead. I just couldn't cope." He turned away, hiding the tears that were only just managing to stay in his eyes.

"What on earth do you mean? It was all fine. I just took longer to come around than usual."

"No Perse, it wasn't like that. Look the parents don't think it's a good idea to tell you but you have to know that you really were out cold. It was a million times worse than in the market. Even your grandma was scared and I didn't think I'd ever see that. Even our parents don't really know how bad it was. They weren't there and I was."

They walked in silence for a while.

"Sorry." A quiet little voice from Persi.

"'s al'right." An equally quiet voice from Danny and they turned and walked home in a slightly more companionable silence.

A few hours later they were back around grandma's table doing justice to a leg of lamb with all the trimmings. There was a lot of conversation about local affairs, what was happening at school, what were they going to do about getting the twins Christened. In fact, they spoke about everything except what was on everyone's mind. What was Persi going to do next?

It was after all the dishes had been washed and put away and the twins had been fed and were enjoying a kick around on the floor with Daisy banned to the garden since she couldn't help trying to lick them and roll around with them, that Persi finally bought the subject up.

"Grandma, could I have Rita's phone number? I think I need to talk things through with her."

The adults looked at each other and Danny looked suddenly interested in the view out of the window.

"Do you think that's a good idea?" asked her mum.

"Yes, actually I think it's the best way forward. I need to know if there's anything else I need to do before trying again." She looked around at the others. "I know what you're all thinking but I can do this. I know I can. I'm not going to leave that poor boy where he is and I'm just trying to ensure that I'm doing everything possible to keep myself safe."

They were all struck by how mature she sounded. She wasn't reacting like a moody teenager trying to get her own way, she was reasoning it out like an adult. Despite the misgivings they all felt her mum gave her grandma a quiet nod and grandma went to the sideboard and wrote down a number from her phone book and gave it to Persi.

"Thank you." Persi smiled around at everyone, lighting up the room. "Would now be a good time to call do you think?"

"Well she had an answer machine so you can always leave a message."

"Great, I'll ring now then you can all check to see what I'm saying." The others all looked a bit guilty, but were all relieved that they would get some idea of what was happening.

The phone rang. "Hi Rita, it's Persi." "Yes I'm fine thanks, but I had a bit of a strange experience yesterday when I used the ring and I wonder if there's anything else I can do to help myself," "Right, yes, I know, OK that's fine, Thanks so much, I expect grandma will be ringing you soon. Yes, I will. Thanks again, bye"

Persi looked around at everyone. They all looked expectantly at her.

"I don't think any of you are going to like this but she says I was to believe in myself and to remember that where there's hope there's life. Oh and she sends her love."

"What the hell does that mean?" Danny blurted out angrily.

"What did you say to me that brought me around?" Persi asked Danny.

Looking around at the others guiltily, he replied. "Hope needs you, remember Hope."

"There you are then. I continue to do all that I've already been doing, and if you are worried about me then just remind me of Hope." She smiled down at her little sister, so much smaller than her brother but equally determined to enjoy the play session. "I love all of you but Hope is somehow special to me. I'll never leave her. You don't have to worry about me." She laughed, "well not more than you can help."

"I don't want you going up there again Persi." Said her mum. "You're so far from help. I can see you're determined to do this and so if you do I want you to do it here, where we're all around you and Hope is next to you."

Persi reached down and picked up the little girl who was beginning to tire, she tucked her into her arm looked down and found those huge bright blue eyes looking into hers and smiled.

"That's fine by me."

Chapter 21

The next day was school again and she and Neda were once again together and it was lunch break. They tended to spend the time in the library usually, but today was lovely after the awful weather of Saturday so they decided to walk around the sports field. They were at the far perimeter when a cricket ball, hit by an enthusiastic but unskilled third year came flying towards them with no warning and hit Neda on the side of the head.

She went down like a sack of potatoes and the boys who'd been practicing their cricket came running over yelling. "Is she OK?" "Sorry, I didn't mean to." "Is she dead?"

Persi was down by her friend's side immediately. She looked up at the boys and yelled at them to go and tell a member of staff. While they were running back towards the school, Persi knelt and put her hands on Neda's head where the ball had hit. It was easy to find the spot as there was a cut that was bleeding profusely and a huge lump was already forming. Persi breathed deeply and concentrated on her friend and felt the familiar and comforting strength flowing from her body through her hands and into Neda. She didn't consider that it wouldn't work, she knew it would, and as long as she kept this faith all would be well. Neda stirred and muttered. "Ow, what hit me, my head hurts."

"Don't worry, you'll be fine. Just stay still and let me help you."

Neda appeared to recognise the authority in Persi's voice and stayed still.

"Mmm, it's not hurting as much now. It feels all warm and nice somehow."

"Good, just stay still until someone comes."

Within moments two teachers came over and said an ambulance had been called for. The boys had been so afraid of what they'd done that they'd given a very clear explanation of what had happened but had said that Neda was unconscious. However it was evident that she was fully conscious now because she was trying to sit up. Persi was calmly telling her to stay still.

By the end of the lunchtime, Neda had been taken off to hospital to be checked over, Moj had been told what had happened to his sister and word had got all around the school that Persi had saved Neda's life. Danny came to find her but she was in the medical bay washing the blood off her hands and trying to clean it off her uniform.

Afternoon lessons went on as usual but every time Persi had to move from one class to another she found everyone looking at her and trying to ask her what had happened. It didn't help that the boys who'd caused all the trouble were now more or less saying that Neda had been dead and Persi had bought her back to life.

Then someone remembered the newspaper articles about her saving her sisters life after the birth and suddenly Persi found herself in the centre of some very unwanted attention.

Waiting for their bus Danny sidled up to her and whispered, "Just as well they don't know the half of it," She turned to him and didn't know whether to hit him or laugh. She grinned and whispered back. "You wait, I'll get you back for that."

When she got to grandma's she had to explain what had happened while they soaked her uniform in cold water hoping to remove some of the bloodstains until they could replace it.

It wasn't long before Neda's parents came around to thank Persi for her help and to tell her that Neda was coming home once the results of the scans were back, but it didn't look as if there was any real damage.

Then Robbie and her mum came over to check that she was OK.

By the time she had managed to get rid of everyone and have something to eat she was exhausted and went to bed early without touching her homework, a first for her.

She slept for a few hours and then awoke very early in the morning. Lying in bed she wished she was on the boat so that she could open the front hatch and look out at the canal. The view wasn't quite as good now that she was in the boatyard, but she liked having water under and around her. It balanced her somehow. Much as she loved her grandma and enjoyed the weeks with her, she suddenly really missed the boat. Sighing she turned over and thought over all the events of yesterday and then about Willem and fell into a restless sleep to be woken by grandma wondering why she was still in bed.

She felt she couldn't face school today and asked grandma to ring in and say that she was feeling ill after the events of the day before and that she'd be back the next day.

Persi couldn't remember having a day off school before, she probably had when she was younger and she was proud of her 100% attendance record but today she just couldn't face it.

After breakfast she rang her mum and told her she wasn't up to school but that she was going to go to the boat and catch up on her homework and chill for the day.

Persi got her bike out and rode back to the boat, taking her time and enjoying being beside the canal. She got to the boat and went straight through to open the front hatch and sat there gazing at the water, listening to the sounds of the boatyard and grounding herself.

She did her homework and then some research for a project she had been planning. At lunch time she went in the house and had lunch with her mum and Robbie and cuddled Hope while her mum was feeding George.

"Mum, I've made a decision. I want to train as a midwife when I leave school. I've been thinking about it for a while and I know that I'd be good at it."

"That's a brilliant idea, I can vouch for your skills. As soon as you put your hand on my belly I knew that it was all going to be all right. You've got a very calming touch you know."

Persi smiled at her mum, thinking back to that day and then she laughed.

"What's so funny?" her mum asked.

"Rita said I'd be surrounded by babies but not all my own, so that's it then, it's meant to be!"

"Good for you, we'll have to look into it and see what subjects you need to do." She paused, "Persi, you know I'm very proud of you don't you?" Persi nodded. "But I'm really worried about this whole ring thing. I'm not trying to stop you." Seeing Persi's expression change, she quickly reacted. "I just don't know how I'd cope if anything happened to you."

"It's OK mum, I'm fine, I've got it all sorted. I've decided that the next time we go to grandma's I'm going to try again. I've already proved I'm able to do it, and next time I'll succeed. I promise. And once I've got Willem safe there won't be a ring anymore so you won't have to worry."

With that she reached over and gave her mum an unexpected kiss on the cheek. Then she got up and put the now sleeping Hope in her pram and went into the kitchen to make a cup of tea for them both.

Chapter 22

School the next day was as bad as Persi had feared. She was the centre of attention and even Abby appeared to want to be seen with her. Neda was back home and fine but told that she should stay at home for a few days to rest. She had rung Persi that morning before school and told her she felt well, and that she'd rather be at school. She was worrying about what work she might be missing so Persi had promised to go over that evening to fill her in.

Persi was so used to being an inconspicuous member of class, working steadily and getting good marks but never the centre of anything, that she now felt very uncomfortable with the attention that the others were showing her. Even some of the members of staff were treating her differently.

'How long is this going to last' she asked herself. Having a horrible feeling that until something else came along to take the attention off her, she'd be a novelty.

At the end of the morning she was called into the head teachers office.

"I'd just like to say how grateful we are as a school for your swift action the other day. I understand that Neda apparently was knocked out and had a bad head-wound but your swift attention and care appear to have meant that she's enjoying a very swift recovery." Mr. Unwin was a good bloke but could come over as a bit formal, and Persi wasn't sure how to deal with it. Feeling it was best to be honest, she looked straight at him.

"Thank you sir, but I only kept her quiet and I'm sure that anyone else would have done the same. Er… is it possible to make people stop treating it as a big deal? I'm really uncomfortable at having everyone looking at me, and pointing me out."

She gave him a steady but slightly desperate look.

He laughed. "I shall do what I can but you ought to be proud of yourself, the staff are very grateful to your quick thinking. It could have had a very different outcome. Don't be embarrassed that you've done a good thing."

"No sir, thank you sir."

"All right, off you go but keep your head high."

She came out of the office and found Danny waiting for her. He took one look at her and walked her off to the canteen where he found a quiet table and bought her a cold drink and a bun.

"You're always filling me with buns and drinks, do you know that?"

"Well it seems to be necessary, you keep getting yourself in these situations. I saw Moj and he says that Neda thinks you are some sort of angel."

"Oh no, that's all I need. I'm going over to see her tonight, so I'll try to be horrible and evil so that she changes her mind."

"Yeah, right, like that's going to happen. You've just got to accept that you're a good person Persi Stone. That's a point, are you going to keep your name or do you think you ought to change it to Jamison? Now that your mum and my dad are married you're the only one with a different name, how do you feel about it?"

Persi was surprised, she hadn't given a thought to it, but now it had been mentioned she realised that it would be nice to be the same as the rest of her family. Danny was probably the best big brother in the world, and if he wanted to make it more official maybe she ought to.

"I'll talk it over with mum, but I honestly hadn't thought about it. Do you think I ought to?"

"It'd be good I think. There's two sisters and two brothers and I reckon they ought to have the same name."

At that the bell went so they disappeared in different directions to afternoon classes.

That evening she went to visit Neda, complete with some work that she'd got from her day off and hoped that this would be enough to keep her happy for a bit. When she arrived at the house, Neda's mum welcomed her at the door with a huge hug and a big smile. She showed Persi through into the living room and Neda was sat on the settee with a bandage around her head.

"Persi, it's so good to see you. It seems ages."

"Only a couple of days, glad to see you looking so well." She went and hugged Neda and was surprised at the strength that Neda hugged her back with.

"What did you do? Don't say you just kept me calm, I know the pain I was in and I know it felt better after you'd touched my head."

Neda looked at her with big brown eyes, filled with tears that she was trying not to shed.

"I didn't do anything."

"Yes you did, you know you did. I haven't said anything to anyone else but I know that you stopped it from being much worse than it was. I think you're my guardian angel." She laughed and wiped her eyes.

They looked at each other and Persi decided that she had to trust her. She didn't want to tell her the whole story but simply said that she'd discovered that she'd inherited healing powers that she could use when needed. Neda wanted to know more naturally, so Persi explained that her great-grandmother had been considered a wise woman, as was her mother before her and that it seemed that the healing powers had come down through her grandma and mum to her.

Neda nodded as she listened to the explanation and at the end took hold of Persi's hand.

"I'll always be grateful to you. I know how much good you can do but I promise I'll never say anything. I'd heard that Abby tried to tell everyone that you thought you could do magic last year and what a baby you were. If only she realised how clever you are, she might have been a bit more careful about what she said."

Persi was hurt to find that the stories that Abby had told were still in people's minds but realised that in Neda she really did have a true friend.

After another big hug, Persi explained to Neda what work was being done at school and they spent a little time looking through their text books at the next exercises, then Persi left to go back for tea at grandma's, but not before Neda's mum had enveloped her in another huge hug and thanked her again.

Persi wasn't sure what Mr. Unwin had said but over the next few days she noticed that people weren't quite as interested in her. Maybe that was just time going past but whatever it was Persi was happier to be out of the limelight.

She spoke to her mum about the change of name and they decided that it would be a nice thing to do, and Robbie was delighted. Persi said she didn't want to give up her name entirely and how would Stone-Jamieson sound? After trying it out loud a few times, Donna agreed it was a good idea. Robbie gave her a big hug when they told him and said that now he really did have two daughters.

Danny smiled at her and she knew what it meant to him, which made it all worthwhile.

Chapter 23

Then it was Sunday and they were at grandma's house for lunch again.

Once again they sat around after the meal and Persi asked for the first time.

"So who's got the ring then?"

Grandma went over to the sideboard and found the box.

"Danny had it in his pocket for a couple of days before we remembered it, strangely enough. Here it is, safe and sound."

Persi had been very careful to do her meditation despite everything that had gone on at school that week and had her 'bag of luck' with her. After the last time she had put it on a strong cord around her neck so that it was easy to hold on to if she needed it.

Grandma had prepared the tea and added plenty of honey so that it was easy to drink and Persi dutifully drank it without making a face as she was very aware of everyone watching her. It felt a bit weird to have them all there, like she was some sort of sideshow. She didn't like it at all but if this is what it took then she had to do it.

She took the ring and smiled around at everyone then her mum said. "Hang on." And she moved over onto the settee next to Persi holding Hope in her arms. "Hope is going to be right next to you and we want to put something else in your bag." She quickly reached into her pocket and bought out a few very sparse and fair hairs. "These are from Hope and well…we just want you to have them."

Persi was close to tears but slipped the hairs into the bag and nodded to her mum unable to speak as she slipped the ring onto her finger.

The cold hit her as soon as she realised she was back in the clearing. This was the last thing she'd wanted; she'd hoped to just find herself in the forest as she was sure that Willem would find her.

The cause of the chill didn't seem to be there. No apparition or that dreadful laugh. Neither were there any children there so whatever she'd done on her previous visit was permanent. This was something to be grateful for.

She looked around and wondered if she'd be able to get out of the clearing, but then remembered that it was while she was trying to do this last time was when the…. whatever it was, turned up.

A stone suddenly landed next to her, close enough to make her jump, she started to turn in the direction it had come from.

"Don't turn around, she may be watching you."

It was Willem's voice, and she hoped that it was him and not some sort of trick. Anything could happen in this place.

"Is that you Willem?"

"Course it is, who else is it likely to be?"

"I don't know, what was your mum's name?"

"Hilde."

"OK, how did you find me?"

"It wasn't hard, SHE makes a lot of noise and I know this place and I guessed that she'd bring you here. Why weren't you more careful?

"I couldn't find you, and I knew not to call out so I just started walking, hoping to find you."

Suddenly there was a horrible laugh, one that Persi recognised, and this time she was far more scared because she realised what had probably happened.

"I have you, at last I have you. You vermin, thinking you can hide from me forever. I set my trap well didn't I?"

The laughter became more and more unbearable and suddenly Willem was in the centre of the clearing with bonds around him. Unlike Persi, his bonds seemed to be more permanent and Persi felt tears in her eyes. It was her fault that Willem was here. If she hadn't come back for him he'd have continued to hide and still be free.

Then she thought, 'No, I'm here to help him, I want to release him, so that he can return to Eyam and then he can be at rest.'

Persi went towards him, but couldn't get close, the same power that stopped her getting out of the clearing seemed to be stopping her from reaching him. Frustrated Persi cried out to Willem.

"Don't worry, I'm going to save you, believe me."

The laughter started again.

"You, little girl, do you believe that you are stronger than me? Are you really THAT arrogant? No-one escaped from me, this is my kingdom, my wishes are the law here. You, you are nothing, do you hear NOTHING!" The laughter disappeared slowly into the forest.

"You're wrong, I helped the others escape, you know I did. I'm stronger than you. You only know pain and fear, I know healing and love. I'll always win." She screamed this into the air, and she saw Willem cringing, she'd obviously scared him.

As she watched she saw him change. The fear in his face disappeared and was replaced by a lifeless gazing into the distance and he didn't seem aware of her any more. He had the same expressionless face that the other children had. Persi tried to run towards him but once again found her legs struggling to get close enough to touch him.

Worried that she wasn't going to be able to do any more without thinking this through she wondered if she ought to take the ring off and leave, or whether it would be better to stay. Looking at Willem she realised she couldn't leave him like this, it would be like breaking a promise so she sat down on the ground, took some deep breaths and tried to think what to do.

She reasoned that if she left she may not be able to get back to this clearing again, and that wouldn't help Willem at all, so somehow she had to get to him. At the moment it seemed as if she couldn't get closer than an arm's length towards him and he didn't seem to be able to respond to her.

She started thinking and the ideas were going around in circles until she had a clear thought that came from no-where. 'None of this is real, it's all in Willems mind, so all you have to do is to snap him out of his belief in it all and you'll be able to reach him.'

Still she argued with herself and realised that the longer that she left it, the more likely the Shape as she'd started to think of it, could return and start to amuse herself with them. Persi had no idea what this might mean but it didn't sound pleasant.

She got up and went as close to Willem as she could get.

"Willem, Willem, listen to me, can you hear me?"

There didn't seem to be any response from the boy.

"Willem, this is really important. You MUST listen to me."

Persi concentrated her mind to focus totally on the boy stood in front of her, completely lifeless. She reached her hands out towards him and willed the power that she had felt before when she was helping reduce pain and tried to channel it towards him.

For several minutes nothing happened and then Persi felt rather than saw a change in him.

"That's it Willem, hear me, FEEL me, can you feel me touching you?"

A slight nod was all Persi needed.

"Good boy, now reach your hands out to me."

Like an automaton he raised his hands and their fingers touched.

"In a minute I want you to take your mum's ring off my finger but continue to hold my other hand. Can you do that?"

Another slight nod.

"Good boy, you're doing so well, right are you ready?"

She felt him grip the ring but then there was that awful laughter filling the whole clearing.

"You are proving to be more annoying rather than amusing girl. What are you doing, he's mine?"

"He's NOT" Persi screamed. "You are just something evil in his imagination. Fear of you had kept him here for all this time. You don't exist, do you hear me, you DON'T EXIST. NOW Willem, NOW"

The ring left Persi's finger and she found herself back in her grandma's living room, sat on the settee with Hope's toes resting on her arm.

"Thank heavens you're safe, is all well?"

Grandma was concerned as Persi struggled to realise what had happened.

Grandma was the first to speak. "Did you succeed? What happened? The ring suddenly disappeared from your finger and then opened your eyes again."

Danny nodded, "Yes it was really weird, you were only out a few seconds, where's the ring?"

Persi took a deep breath.

"Well I think it all went well, Willem and I held hands and he took the ring off and we left the forest. It wasn't real, it was all in his imagination. I was right, it must have been his idea of hell, searching endlessly through a dense forest for his mum, being pursued by a scary apparition and imagining other children being caught and tortured. It's pretty scary stuff, especially for a young boy. He took the ring and hopefully now is at peace with him mum."

At that she burst into tears. Tears of relief that she was back safely, tears of sorrow for the pain that Willem had been suffering and tears of joy that it was all over.

It seemed to be a bit of an anti-climax somehow, there was nothing to show for her efforts and no-one but her had any idea of what had really happened, and worst of all she could only suppose that all had ended well for Willem.

Grandma and Danny kept supplying her with tissues until the flood eventually dried up.

"I could really do with a cup of something warm and something to eat,"

"Persi, you've just had a huge meal." Exclaimed her mum.

"She's always like this, give her a bun and a cup of tea and all is well again." Danny laughed, making his way to the kitchen.

"No, I'll do it." Grandma said, "I've made a cake especially as I thought it might be needed."

Persi was looking down at her finger. "The ring's gone. I sort of knew it had gone with Willem in the other place, but I didn't know if it would still be here."

"Thank goodness for that." Exclaimed her mum. "Now it's gone we can settle down to just being an ordinary family."

"Do you really believe that?" Asked Danny. "I don't reckon you know your elder daughter all that well." He looked at Persi and laughed. Gradually the rest of the family joined in. Persi looked down and Hope was smiling her first real smile.

Printed in Great Britain
by Amazon